Advance Praise for
Things That Shimmer

"A nuanced and beautiful story about the transformative power of true friendship: the power to strip away and the power to build anew. I loved it!"

—Evan Wolkenstein, author of *Turtle Boy*

"A heartwarming middle grade novel about friendship and all its complications, set in the shadow of the Watergate scandal and the Yom Kippur War. Lovely!"

—Tziporah Cohen, author of *No Vacancy*

"Between the casual and uncomplicated Jewish backdrop, the rich period detail and pitch-perfect cultural touchstones, the sensitive rendering of a young teen with a traumatized parent, and the highly relatable crucible-like setting of middle school social climbing and cliques, I could not stop turning the pages of *Things That Shimmer*. But it was the nuanced and complicated friendships that really stood out for me, keeping me thinking about Mel, Dorit, Vicky, and Marla long after I turned the last page. How I would have loved to read this book when I was growing up! How I loved it now!"

—Meira Drazin, author of *Honey and Me*, a 2023 Sydney Taylor Honor Book and Kirkus Best Middle Grade Book of 2022

"Deborah Lakritz perceptively captures the destructive power of cool-girl cliques in this sensitive middle grade novel. Adolescents everywhere will identify with Melanie's poignant struggle to be both popular and true to herself."

—Jacqueline Jules, award-winning author of *My Name Is Hamburger*, *The Hardest Word*, and *Picnic at Camp Shalom*

"Like Judy Blume before her, Deborah Lakritz navigates a teen girl's world with a deft hand and a warm heart. Readers will cheer for Melanie and worry for her from page one, as she rides the roller coaster that is adolescence. Combining authentic Jewish representation with an engaging story of friendships lost and found, *Things That Shimmer* shows kids that it's okay to make mistakes and sometimes say the wrong thing, and that everyone needs support from those they love, even moms and dads."

—Stacy Nockowitz, author of *The Prince of Steel Pier*

"Deborah Lakritz shows the importance of understanding who you are—and who your friends are—in this story about growing up and being brave."

—Madelyn Rosenberg, author of *One Small Hop* and coauthor of *Not Your All-American Girl*

"A realistic and moving portrait of a young girl's yearning to fit in as she tiptoes through the landmines of middle school and a troubled home life, setting her on a path to uncover what truly matters."

—Betsy R. Rosenthal, author of *When Lightnin' Struck* and *Looking for Me . . . in This Great Big Family*

Things That Shimmer

DEBORAH LAKRITZ

KAR-BEN
PUBLISHING

KAR-BEN PUBLISHING®
An imprint of Lerner Publishing Group, Inc.
241 First Avenue North
Minneapolis, MN 55401 USA

Website address: www.karben.com

Cover illustration by Lara Paulussen.

Main body text set in Bembo Std.
Typeface provided by Monotype Typography.

Library of Congress Cataloging-in-Publication Data

Names: Lakritz, Deborah, author. | Paulussen, Lara, 1988– illustrator.
Title: Things that shimmer / Deborah Lakritz ; [illustrated by Lara Paulussen].
Description: Minneapolis, MN : Kar-Ben Publishing, [2024] | Audience: Ages 8–12. | Audience: Grades 4–6. | Summary: Set in 1973, Melanie desperately wants to be accepted by the Shimmers, the popular girls in her class, but when she gets to know Dorit, the new girl from Israel, she must choose between popularity and true friendship.
Identifiers: LCCN 2023004411 (print) | LCCN 2023004412 (ebook) | ISBN 9781728476261 (hardcover) | ISBN 9798765613559 (epub)
Subjects: CYAC: Popularity—Fiction. | Friendship—Fiction. | Middle schools—Fiction. | Schools—Fiction. | Jews—United States—Fiction. | LCGFT: Historical fiction. | Novels.
Classification: LCC PZ7.L15934 Th 2024 (print) | LCC PZ7.L15934 (ebook) | DDC [Fic]—dc23

LC record available at https://lccn.loc.gov/2023004411
LC ebook record available at https://lccn.loc.gov/2023004412

Manufactured in China
1-52208-50648-5/30/2023

To Ronit, of course.

Chapter 1

IT'S FUNNY HOW THOSE OLD SAYINGS YOU HEAR over and over are sometimes the exact truth.

Dad has said, "The grass is always greener on the other side" more times than I can count. He used it on me when I was nine, after I begged to return my Hanukkah present, a paint-by-numbers set, in exchange for an Easy-Bake Oven like the one my best friend, Vicky, got from her parents.

He could say it this morning too—and lots of mornings—about the way I sit watching the Shimmers stake their territory at the flagpole before first bell rings.

I escaped the house this morning without any predictions of doom from Mom, I'm holding the bag of chocolate-drizzled macaroons I baked last night, and the April sun catches the sequins dotting my new shirt. I should be feeling happy, but I can't shift my eyes away from the only people who matter at Ashford Junior High.

The Shimmers are bonded together like a golden fence surrounds them. They only let in the people they think deserve to be there. They've even claimed special places everyone knows are only for them: the center tables in the cafeteria, the last row in the auditorium, and the flagpole.

Some girls from my typing class wave as they pass, and I smile when a neighborhood kid calls my name, but no one stops to sit down with me. And Vicky isn't here yet, of course. For our whole lives, she's never made it to school before the Pledge of Allegiance. Besides, I'm not even sure if she'd come sit with me or dart straight over to the flagpole to be with the Shimmers. That's how it is between us these days.

"Give it back, you thieves!" Shari Kaye, the actual queen of seventh grade, swipes the air to grab her hat from the boys. Marla Forstein and Jan Rosen, who stand on either side of Shari, look like they waltzed straight off the pages of *Teen Beat*, all cool and confident. Aaron Andrews flings Shari's hat up into the air, and it catches on a tree branch near where I'm sitting. "Oh, great!" she says. "How am I supposed to get it down?"

Everyone looks at me. I've climbed this tree hundreds of times, but never with an all-star audience. "I . . . I guess I can get it." My face sizzles as I hoist myself up and give the branch a shake. When Shari's hat plops to the ground, I watch and wait, imagining how she's going to smile and say thanks and ask me my name (again), and I'll make a joke about being part mountain goat, and maybe we'll laugh together.

But she doesn't.

She jogs off, rosy cheeks and twinkly eyes, tugging the floppy rim over her head. Everyone follows like she's the grand marshal of the Tournament of Shimmers parade. It's a *thwack* straight to my gut like the time Jon and I wrestled in the living room and he accidentally kneed me in the stomach. I'm glad Vicky isn't here to see me pretend I'm okay.

As the bell rings and I slink into school, I can't help thinking that if the Shimmers wanted me, I could be somebody new.

Mom's worries wouldn't get under my skin anymore. Even if she circled the neighborhood in a panic (again) when I was late coming home from school, I'd brush it off instead of feeling guilty, as if I'd done something wrong.

No one else has a mom like mine, and even though I try to act like everything's normal, most of the time it's not. But being a Shimmer would be even *better* than normal; it would be perfect.

The first bell rings, and I hustle down the crowded hall until I reach homeroom. While kids chatter, I whip out a diagram to test myself on the parts of a typewriter for this afternoon's quiz. I studied all last night because tests make me so nervous. Before I can find the carriage release lever, the wall speaker crackles.

"*Good morning! Lunch is tater tot casserole, tropical fruit cup, and milk,*" spits a student announcer whose mouth must be stuck to the microphone. "*Track-and-field practice meets at 3:45 sharp. Shortwave Radio Club still needs members; impress friends and family by communicating with people all over the globe!*"

I find the last two typewriter parts, the paper bail and the backspacer.

"And finally, Melanie Adler, report directly to Miss Roole after homeroom."

"Ooh, Adler! Miss Model Student!" Jerry Finkel's hands drum the top of my desk. "You're in trouble," he singsongs. "What did ya do, anyway—ditch a class?"

My heart springs to my throat. I jump out of my seat, the typewriter diagram sailing to the floor. Without waiting for the official end of homeroom, I race out the door, passing some kids with late passes and a bubble-lettered poster of Snoopy that screams *Pounce on Pollution!*

I wince thinking about Jerry's taunt. I *have* become big on rule following ever since our accident. I don't tattle on other kids or act like I'm better—I just hate getting in trouble because that's one more thing Mom has to worry about. Kids like Jerry figure this means all my grades are perfect, but lots of nights Dad has to explain my math homework for the bazillionth time. I'm so glad he's patient—about everything.

Around the corner, a boy's pushing the coin return buttons on the pay phones along the wall, checking to see if he can get any change. When he sees me, he shrugs. "No luck today."

Isn't that the truth.

Miss Roole and her immovable hair meet me under the sign that says *Vice Principal*. She's not giving away any clues about why she sent for me—her mouth's a straight line that could've been drawn by a cartoonist.

I follow her past secretaries filing attendance cards and the framed portrait of President Nixon. The atmosphere is more funeral parlor than school office. Other than the sound of the mimeograph machine humming out copies, it's silent. *Why am I here?*

"Have a seat, Miss Adler," she says, taking me into her office. She pushes away a desk calendar—*1973: A Year of Motivational Quotes*. The message for April is "Every problem has a gift for you in its hands." She hoists herself up on the cleared space, as if there's a chance she could look casual.

A girl I've never seen before sits on a flimsy chair next to Miss Roole's desk. She flips through the school handbook and nods at me.

5

"Melanie Adler, meet Dorit Shoshani. Today she joins our community of learners. I've chosen *you* to show her around." Dorit smooths the hair over her ears and tightens her long ponytail. It's the color of the toffee Dad used to bring home from work conferences. Back when he could still go out of town without Mom freaking out that his plane was going to crash or his hotel was going to burn down. Back before the accident.

My body's drenched with relief. I'm not in trouble. Miss Roole chose me!

For once it actually pays to be a "model student." I get to know something before anyone else in school— even before the Shimmers.

Miss Roole launches into what my grandma would call "a whole spiel" about our award-winning school, while Dorit rests the student handbook on the worn-out legs of her jeans. Something tells me she's been through this routine before.

"Blah, blah, discipline . . . blah, blah, hard work . . . blah, blah, courage," Miss Roole says like she's inducting Dorit into the army. It takes forever. But eventually she pats my shoulder and smiles, and I know what's coming.

"Melanie Adler is one of our finest students," she says. "Last year's citizenship award recipient. You're in good hands."

My eyes bore into the ugly green carpeting. Could she make me sound any nerdier? The citizenship award was just a piece of paper with a gold sticker that meant I raised my hand instead of shouting out answers. This girl's going to think I'm the biggest loser.

After more blabbing about our accelerated curriculum, Miss Roole finally leads us to the deserted hallway. I pull Dorit away before she can hear something else that makes me sound even weirder, but Miss Roole keeps calling after us. "I know you've attended schools all over the world, but it never hurts to have a helping hand. It's what makes Ashford Junior High special." I half expect the cheerleading squad to pop up behind her and burst into our school song.

When we're safely past the office, homeroom's long over and first period is about to end. "Let's find your locker before the halls are packed," I say. We hurry past the Girls' Foods room where the smell of cinnamon wafts over us.

"Is Miss Roole always that serious?" Dorit asks, hiding a grin.

"Yeah, her nickname is The Ruler. Rumor has it she can recite the entire Constitution by heart."

Dorit's laugh is soft and wheezy. "She sure likes you. Citizenship award—"

"Never mind that," I say, shutting her down. I don't

need another person thinking I'm prissy and perfect. She doesn't even know me yet.

She gets it right away. "Don't worry; in sixth grade I won the Student Visionary award. Sounds like I tell fortunes, right?" We both crack up.

"Sorry," she says after a few coughs. "Allergies. They've been bugging me since we moved here." As Dorit adjusts her ponytail, I smile. Something about her seems so familiar. Maybe it's the freckles; we both have a ton. I wonder if she hates hers as much as I hate mine.

Dorit's cuffed bell-bottoms drag under her sneakers as we pass rows of lockers. "Here's 234," she says, like she's done this a gazillion times. Sticking to the metal door is a strip of masking tape with *Dorit Shoshani* printed in marker. She peels the tape off and rolls it into a ball.

"Doh-*reet*. That's so pretty," I say.

She shrugs. "My mom told me it means 'of this generation.' I hate it. It's Hebrew. I was born in Israel." Her words have a soft clipped sound. Not an obvious accent, but a little different.

"You just moved here from *Israel*?" I shift my books to my hip. Pictures from Sunday school pop into my head: soldiers, tanks, people working in fields, and maps with dotted lines for borders that our teacher said are always changing.

"No, I was *born* there. We moved away when I was little; I barely remember it because we've lived in so many other places."

"Oh," I say. "How come you left?"

"Lots of reasons."

Her eyes won't meet mine anymore, so I know something's up. New kids don't just show up in spring when the school year is practically over. Not unless they have to. It makes me super curious and I almost ask her about it, but I know better. After our car accident, people always butted in with personal questions about Mom, like why she was wearing an eye patch or why she stayed inside all the time, like it was even their business. I don't want Dorit to think I'm like that too.

"Hey," I say to change the subject, "Here's *my* locker. There's a math folder somewhere under this heap of junk." I swing the door open and scoop up a pile of old homework papers until I see the bottom. "Can I interest you in a fossilized lunch?"

Her smile comes back. I even make her laugh. "I guess they don't check how neat you are before they hand out the citizenship award, huh?"

It's my turn to laugh. "I'm good at staying out of detention, but I'll never get a blue ribbon for tidiness." The end of the first period bell rings as I click my lock closed. "Ahem. Ready for math, Miss Visionary?"

"I sense a fascinating morning ahead, Miss Citizenship," Dorit says, pressing her fingers to the sides of her head.

News travels fast in seventh grade, and by lunchtime everyone knows about "the new girl who's lived all over the world."

At my usual spot off to the side of the cafeteria, something keeps me from pulling out my chair. It kills me that I can't lead Dorit over to the Shimmers' table in the center, plop down like it's no big deal, and say, "Oh, by the way, this is Dorit. She's new here." As soon as she sees them, she's going to wonder how she got stuck here with me instead.

But we dump our books on the floor and she digs into her lunch bag all casual, like she doesn't even notice who the cool kids are and where they're sitting.

I've barely unwrapped my sandwich when the visits to our table begin.

Lisa and Charlene, gossipy neighborhood kids I've known my whole life, are first up. "You're really from Israel?"

Dorit takes a long sip from her juice can before she responds. "Yeah. Jerusalem. Have you been there?"

Lisa shakes her head. "My parents say it's way too dangerous. Aren't there always wars there?"

Pink splotches dot Dorit's neck.

"Come on," says Charlene. "Let's eat."

As they walk away, Lisa turns around. "*Leh-heet-rah-ote*—see you later," she says, drawing out the word with a giggle. "That's all I learned in Hebrew school."

A moment later, Shari and Marla cruise up to our table. My heart jumps as I bite into my bologna sandwich.

"Hi! I'm Shari, and this is Marla—Are you Doreen?"

Dorit presses her lips together to stifle a laugh, but I swallow hard. They pay even less attention to me now than they did in front of school this morning.

"Doh-*reet*," she says. "My parents' fault. No one says it right." You'd have to be living inside a locker to not realize that these are the coolest girls in seventh grade, but Dorit just flips the top of her yogurt container and keeps eating.

"Seats, ladies." Mrs. Dooley, the lunch monitor, frowns.

"We're only staying for a second." Shari scans the cafeteria, then lowers herself to the edge of one of our empty seats as if she doesn't want to sit on something gross. She signals Marla toward the other one. I take in every detail: Marla's green cat-eyes and straight dancer posture. Shari's dimpled smile and that floppy hat that people thought was weird the first time she wore it. (But then everyone went out and bought one, of course.) They're both wearing jeans that are faded to powder blue and embroidered around the pockets. I rub my hands over my new cardboard-stiff ones that'll need a dozen washes to soften up like theirs. I saw their outfits hanging in the window of a shop in downtown Ashford. When I asked to go inside, Mom made one of her *I'm-not-wasting-my-money-there* faces. She insists on buying my clothes at Katt and Company, where you get what you pay for.

As Marla's fingers glide through her smooth locks, I pat my own curly layers. Why is my hair such a puff-ball today? Dorit spoons through her yogurt, barely noticing when Shari plunks her tanned arms on the table, clinking her row of bangle bracelets.

"So where do you live?" Shari asks. "I usually know when someone new moves in 'cause my mom is Sandy Kaye, the Ready Realtor. I'll bet she sold you your house."

Dorit gulps her juice and covers a burp with her hand. "We're renting an apartment for now. My mom says the houses here lack character."

I stop chewing and try to catch Dorit's eye before she offends the Shimmers. I tap my fingers on our table. Clear my throat. Blink at her until my eyes bug. But she licks her spoon without noticing my warnings.

"Tell your parents to check out Highland Hills," says Shari. "That's where we live." Along with the rest of the Shimmers. Shari looks Dorit up and down with her sure Shimmer eye. "So, what'd you do at your old school?"

Dorit answers all matter-of-fact, like she doesn't care about impressing them. "School paper and junior debate team." She dips a hunk of bread into a container of something creamy.

"Guess who!" a voice snorts behind us. Jerry Finkel sneaks up and plants his hands over Shari's eyes.

She wiggles out of his grasp with a fake scowl. "Jerry, I'm gonna kill you!"

"Take it easy, Kaye. Everyone sent me to bring you two back to our table." He shoots me a look. "Hey, how was the principal's office, Miss Model Student?"

My face burns. I'm so tired of that nickname, but it's stuck to me like gum under the typing room desks.

"Guess we'll see you, Dorit," says Shari, shrugging. As she and Marla follow Jerry to their center spot, I overhear him saying, "Her name is Dorito?"

Marla shakes her head and says, "Grow up, Jerry."

Once we're alone, Dorit says, "At my old school, those kids would've been called hotshots. Why do they act like they're better than everyone else?"

I study Dorit's face. I'm relieved they didn't snap

her up and away from me, but mostly I'm confused. "They're the two most popular girls in seventh grade. Couldn't you tell? People would kill to be their friends."

"By 'people,' do you mean you?"

I chew my lip. I've never told anyone—not even Vicky—how much I want to be one of them.

"What makes *them* so special?" asks Dorit. I catch her rolling her eyes.

"It's hard to explain," I say, "but . . . they never look out of place. Everyone wants to be their friend. They're always happy. Or if they get upset, it's because of something small, like their parents won't let them see some movie, not because of anything serious."

Like whether your mom's having another surgery. Or how she asks where you are every five minutes if you're not sitting where she can see you. Or how, even when you are sitting in front of her, she's so focused on the worries running through her head that you might as well be alone.

I don't say any of this to Dorit, but I think it. If I were a Shimmer, I'd never have to worry about belonging anywhere again. Maybe I'd never worry about anything.

"Hotshots. I can spot them a mile away," Dorit says, balling up her lunch bag. "Can you show me where the girls' restroom is?"

We toss our trash and head toward the girls' bathroom. But I feel like I need to do a better job of explaining the situation. "They're not hotshots," I tell Dorit. "They're called the Shimmers. They all live in houses around this lagoon in Highland Hills that people call Shimmer Pond because of how the sun sparkles on it. Everyone's always taking pictures there for weddings and graduations and prom, or whenever there's a reason they're all dressed up. No matter what season, people always say, 'Did you see Shimmer Pond today?'"

"So?"

"So, they're like that too."

We pass a poster of Earth, partially in shadow and hanging alone in the dark sky. It's a super-famous picture called *Earthrise*, taken a few years ago on one of the Apollo space missions.

Pointing to the poster, I say, "It's kind of like when we landed on the moon a few years ago. Did you watch it?"

"Yeah, we lived in England then, in this dinky apartment. We had to borrow someone's TV."

"When I saw Neil Armstrong set foot on the moon, it felt like magic, like he appeared out of nowhere. I'll never forget it. At first, the screen was dark and blurry, but then *POOF!* All of a sudden, he climbed out of that spaceship and down the ladder. My brother, Jon, went nuts. Anyway, when I walked into school on the first day of sixth grade, that's what seeing the Shimmers felt like."

"Like an alien invasion?"

"No, like a big important event. They had their nickname before I even found my way to the auditorium for homeroom assignments. Everyone knew they were the cool ones, hanging out in the back row like they owned it." I form an explosion with my fingers. "Like Neil Armstrong on the moon—*poof!* The Shimmers had landed."

Dorit shrugs. "When you've been in as many schools as I have, that whole 'cool group' thing seems pointless. They're not interested in people like me, and I'm not going to run around in circles like a puppy so they'll like me."

She's dead wrong. But I don't want to start an argument since we just met. Instead I pull a brush from my book bag and run it through my hair.

Moving close to the mirror, Dorit changes the subject. "Ugh, I hate my freckles. Wait until summer—I'll have another zillion."

"Yeah. If you haven't noticed, I have a few too." As I scoop my books off the tiled floor, I graze Dorit's math notebook, all of tonight's homework already finished, answers written out in neat little rows.

That's when a girl with swingy blond hair flings open the restroom door and whizzes in past us.

"Oh, hi, Mel! I'm seriously about to burst!" she says in her usual raspy voice. "Doctor's appointment took forever and now everything's blurry from those nasty eyedrops." She slams the stall door. "Gonna be super late for study hall—don't wait."

"Hope you can find your way there," I tease.

"Who's that?" Dorit asks as she follows me out.

"Oh, that's Vicky Rossler, my best friend since we were little."

"She looks like one of those space aliens in the cafeteria."

I shake my head, but the truth is, she's in orbit and ready to land.

Chapter 2

THE WAY DORIT EASES DOWN THE HALL AFTER
only two weeks at school reminds me of the goldfish
I won at our synagogue's Purim carnival last year. At
home, I untied the plastic bag it came in and dumped
the fish into the aquarium on my dresser. After mouth-
ing some pebbles and spitting them back out, that little
fish glimmered and glided around with all the others as
if it had always lived in there. That's Dorit.

"You look worried," she says, eyeing the mess by
my locker, as everyone gets ready to go home. "What's
the matter?"

I rifle through my overstuffed folder. "I can't find
my math homework. And Vicky's late again. And I . . .
I have to get home."

"I'll help you look, but my mom's picking me up
for my allergy shots. She's probably waiting."

My heart jumps as the clock glares from the wall—
3:30. *Yeah, my mom's waiting for me too, in front of our
house, even though it's still too early for me to be home.*

"Look, isn't that it?" Dorit picks up a crinkled sheet of algebra equations.

"Yes! You're a lifesaver!" I stuff the worksheet inside my book bag. "If I only knew how to do them . . ."

Dorit scribbles on a scrap of paper. "Here's my number, *again*. I keep telling you, if your dad's busy, you can call me for help. I already learned it—"

"I know"—I wave—"at your old school."

Dorit disappears into the stairwell. There she is: that little goldfish, darting away.

The locker door presses cold against my back as the clock ticks. I poke my fingers through the holes of my crocheted vest. Mom says I've been waiting for Vicky ever since we met, which I can't even remember because we were both so little. As the story goes, I spotted her playing in her front yard one day as Mom and I walked through our neighborhood. Eventually, whenever we'd pass by her house, I'd wait until she'd come outside so we could play together. The rest is history.

But now everything's so complicated. If I'm five minutes late, Mom starts to worry that something's happened to me. I wish Vicky could understand that and hurry up after school. Sometimes I think about leaving without her, but we promised we'd always wait for each other. As the minutes tick by, I plan the fastest route home: a jog across the park, a shortcut through the Porters' yard, and then straight through the alley-way at the end of our block.

Finally, there's that familiar voice at the end of the hall. "Oh my gosh! You should've come with me!" Vicky's curvy silhouette appears as she bounces past the lockers.

"Where were you?" My hot neck prickles. "My mom's going to go berserk."

"Mel," she says, grabbing me by the shoulders when she reaches me, "Aaron Andrews. Track team. I had to sneak a look." She's hoarse and out of breath—typical Vicky.

"A *look*? I've been waiting by my locker for the past ten minutes so you can stare at today's crush?"

She shakes her head. "This time is different. If only he'd pay attention to me . . ."

The way she bites her cheek can only mean the wheels are spinning inside her head and she's schem-ing for a way to get his attention. Lately everything's a scheme with her. How to distract teachers so they for-get our homework, how to convince her parents that kids in junior high actually get twenty dollars for their allowance . . .

"Here," she says. "I stopped at the school store." She tosses me a bag of my favorite barbecue chips. "I knew you'd be starving."

"You're right," I snap. "I am." But it's awfully hard to stay grumpy with her when she does something nice like that.

"Let's boogie. I promise you won't be late."

We haven't gone far when Jan Rosen leaps toward her, her long hair whipping me in the face. "Bye, V. See ya tomorrow. Isn't track season the best?"

Vicky giggles. "I never knew it could be so fascinating." The knowing look they flash each other makes me feel like a preschooler.

"V?" I ask after Jan breezes down the hall. A pang of jealousy jabs me hard. The Shimmers are noticing Vicky more and more, and it doesn't even seem like she's working that hard to get them to like her.

"Yeah. Some people started calling me V in gym. I think it's cool."

When we were little and all into dress-up and princesses, Vicky made everyone call her Victoria. For all of third grade, she changed it to Tori, after some teenage actress. I'm not surprised that now she's made another switch. But something about this one feels different.

It's like the way we say goodbye to each other, walking home from school every day. As soon as we reach my block we both start drifting backward, in opposite directions toward our own houses so we can still see each other and keep talking. There comes a point where we're getting farther and farther apart, and we can't even hear what the other one's saying anymore, so we both turn around and head to where we're going. I'm scared she's turning around and walking off to become a Shimmer and I'm not. And maybe I never will.

I can't talk about this with her; it's too humiliating that the Shimmers want her but not me. We both know it's true, although neither of us says it out loud. Dad calls stuff like this "the elephant in the room." Too big to ignore, but still, everyone does.

I've told myself to stop worrying. It's *Vicky.* We've always been best friends. But lately, even after I spend a whole day with her, I feel lonely. She's always talking about which boys like her or how she cracks jokes in class and gets sent out to sit in the hall. Half the time I'm not sure if she's even listening to what *I* say.

And lately, when I'm with other seventh graders, I look around and find myself thinking, *Could you be my new best friend?* I had that thought the first time I saw Dorit. When she smiled at me, she looked friendly, not like she was judging me or trying to impress me. And once we started talking, she really listened to what I had to say. If only she weren't so wrong about the Shimmers.

"Good night, ladies," says a stiff voice as we walk

past the principal's office. Miss Roole balances a coffee cup on the mimeograph machine, near a stack of freshly copied papers. The inky smell wafts toward us, and I'll bet if I touched them they'd still be warm. "Any big plans this evening?" she asks, escorting us to the exit.

"Yeah—they're in here." Vicky drags her book bag on the floor. "Doesn't that sound exciting?" She cocks her head to the side and smirks. I'd never talk to Miss Roole like that. And besides, she's not serious. Vicky hasn't done her homework at home in ages. I see her scribbling in between classes.

"How about you, Miss Adler? Plans tonight?"

"I . . . I just have to get home." I give Vicky the eye. Now's not the time to shoot the breeze with the principal.

"Oh, don't be so modest," says Vicky. "You should see her cook."

"You mean, dinner?" Miss Roole asks.

"No, um, for fun." I wish Vicky would stop telling people. It's been months since I checked out *Betty Crocker's New Boys' and Girls' Cookbook* from the school library. The Shimmers happened to walk by just as I brought it to the librarian's desk. Mrs. Carlucci went on and on about some recipe she made from it with her grandkids—canned pears and cottage cheese shaped into bunnies—and I prayed the earth would swallow me up right then and there.

"I won't keep you," says Miss Roole. "Looks like you're in a hurry."

I pull Vicky out the front entrance. "It's 3:50," I say. "If we hustle across the park, I'll only be a few minutes late. Maybe my mom won't even notice."

"You worry too much," she says, and she's right. I'm even grabbing her arm now because we're near a busy street—a reflex since the accident.

"Why'd you tell Miss Roole about my cooking?"

Vicky whips a rock along the park's newly-green grass. "Why not? You're really good at it. Well, except for that sunshine salad. Something must've gone wrong with that one."

No matter how stressed I feel right now, that makes me smile. You wouldn't think a salad made from lemon Jell-O, crushed pineapple, and grated carrots would be toxic, but we both got the worst case of diarrhea from it. Neither of us can mention it now without cracking up.

Vicky gazes across the park, at the baseball field. "Come with me for a second. I have something to show you."

That's "V" talking. Another scheme's coming, and I don't have time for it. The barbecue chips burn in my stomach as I jog-walk ahead. "Vicky, forget it. I'm late—I have to go." The edge of the park is only feet away.

"Wait," she calls after me. "Pleeease?" She runs up behind me and flings her arms around my shoulders. "Come to the bleachers. I want to try something cool that I heard about from Shari and Marla."

My ears tingle when she mentions their names; I can't help it. Man, she knows how to get to me.

"You do realize my mom might be searching for me down every street in the neighborhood by now, right?" And when I finally get home she's going to blame me for worrying her.

"Melanie Adler," says Vicky, pulling me across the baseball field. "You would seriously never have any fun without me."

I heave a breath of surrender. "Let's get this over with."

The afternoon sun twinkles in her eyes. "Are you ready for the blindfold challenge?"

"The what?" My heart skips.

"It's a dare. You do something blindfolded that you're supposed to be super careful about." Vicky covers her eyes and stomps her foot on the metal bench. "I'm gonna climb all the way to the top of the bleachers like this," she says. "Shari jumped off the stage in the auditorium with a bandana over her eyes. She said it felt like she was flying."

"I'm not climbing all the way to the top of the bleachers with my eyes closed."

"*You?* No way! Stand here and watch me. I don't have a bandana, so I need you to be a witness that I kept my eyes closed the whole time."

My heart drums in my chest as she takes a teetering step. There must be fifty rows—and no handrails to keep her from falling off.

She dangles her foot in front of her and taps around for the next step. Her arms extend out to her sides like she's an airplane, inching up, higher and higher.

Leaning too far to one side, she catches herself before she loses her footing. Soon she's way beyond my reach.

"Vicky, be careful!" I want her to hurry, but not if it means falling.

"How am I doing?" she squeals. "Am I almost to the top?" She stretches her toes out in front of her, feeling for the last set of bleachers, but she misses. Arms flailing, she stumbles, slamming her shoulder hard on metal. "Oof!"

"Would you come down now? You're going to fall through to the ground!" I hate how my voice sounds— choked and shaky, like I'm ruining her fun.

When she leaps down from the bleachers, she's rubbing the top of her arm and trying to look like it doesn't hurt, but I know better. "Nothing bad was going to happen to me, you know. Why'd you get so scared?"

"You could've gotten hurt. And I'm going to be late. I already *am* late." This time I'm walking fast, and I don't wait for her.

"Okay, okay," she finally says, running to catch up. "You know, it *is* all right to have fun on your way home."

I'd love to know how that was supposed to be fun.

"Stop looking so worried! You didn't do anything wrong."

She doesn't realize I'm not just worried; I'm *mad*. She never listens to me anymore.

When we reach my block, I jog backward as fast as I can without stumbling over the uneven sidewalk. I'm about to turn around and run home when Vicky stops.

"By the way, I can't sleep over Saturday night. I forgot to tell you. I'm going to Jan's for her birthday."

Suddenly my insides feel hollow and empty. "I've heard about those sleepovers," I say. Sometimes the Shimmers talk in class about prank phone calls they made and all-night Truth or Dare games. And if you're the first to fall asleep, they play tricks on you like dipping your hand in a bowl of warm water to try to make you pee in your sleeping bag.

My back grazes our neighbor's bush. Vicky's figure blends into the houses and trees and lawns. Her voice grows fainter, and if she's saying she's sorry and she'll make it up to me, I don't hear it. I can't make out anything she's saying anymore.

When I turn, Mom's peering out our front window.

I take in the look on her face—a mixture of anger and fear—and a wave of loneliness hits me. I must be the only kid in the world who has to deal with this every day.

Inside, she wraps her arms around me. Instead of launching into an apology and then a whole explanation about why I was late, I reach into my pocket and crinkle the paper scrap with Dorit's phone number on it. Vicky won't be the only one having fun Saturday night.

Chapter 3

SATURDAY AFTERNOON, AN OLD BLACK STATION wagon rumbles into our driveway. I dart from the living room window to turn off my Lickety-Split Hickory Barbecue Sauce sputtering in the kitchen. Once I'm outside, Dorit and her mother step out of their car, leaving two curly-haired boys hanging from the back window. "Bye, Doreetie, sweetie!"

"Never mind them." Dorit rolls her eyes.

Mrs. Shoshani looks like an older version of Dorit: the same oval face and ponytail, with gray streaks running through her hair. Her hazel eyes hold the hint of a smile.

"Thank you for inviting Dorit to sleep over," she says in her thick Israeli accent. "Maybe we'll find a house tomorrow. We're living two weeks already out of boxes."

"Can you come in for a few minutes?" Mom struggles to hold her smile instead of looking down like she usually does when she meets someone new, but Mrs. Shoshani acts like she doesn't even notice

Mom's scarred face. Instead she glances back at the boys in her car.

"I think I should stay here so these two don't fly from the window. After this they need a park. They're . . ." She waves her hands in fast circles, trying to explain. "They're . . ."

"Wild beasts?" offers Dorit.

Mrs. Shoshani lowers her chunky glasses and shoots Dorit a look. "They're full of . . . of meretz."

"She means energy," whispers Dorit.

When I open the door, her brothers yell, "Stay! Don't go yet!"

"Dorit, raq rega—wait a moment while I ask about this house." Mrs. Shoshani points across the street to the brick building with the *FOR SALE* sign in the yard.

"I wouldn't risk it," Mom warns her. "Not with half-dead maple trees so close to the bedrooms. And with all those windows in front, you're just asking for someone to break in." She points down the block. "Look on Mulberry—it's a nice, safe street."

Mrs. Shoshani opens her mouth to say something, but instead, she touches Mom's forearm, like she somehow knows it'll calm her. "Okay," Mrs. Shoshani says. "We'll look someplace else."

Dorit sits really still, taking in everything—Mom's scarred face scrunched in worry, how she stops talking when a siren wails down the street. It's like she sees something's not right with Mom but can't quite piece it together.

I want to disappear. I want Mom to disappear even more.

"Sorry for calling so late yesterday," I whisper to Dorit. I need to distract her before she decides we're too weird and changes her mind about sleeping over. "I'm glad your parents said you could come."

"No kidding. I almost got stuck babysitting those two again." She eyes her brothers, who stretch their mouths wide open with their fingers and stick their tongues out at us.

Our moms step closer to the curb, and Mrs. Shoshani points down the street, but I can't hear what she's saying. I tap my feet. Dorit looks around. I hope it wasn't a mistake to invite her for a whole long sleepover. What if we have nothing to talk about?

Dad's car inches out of the garage, past the Shoshanis' battered station wagon.

"Where are you going?" I call to him.

"Buck's Hardware," he yells through his open window. "I'm picking up sheets of pegboard for the basement."

I think about coming along so I can buy wood and nails for the new string art project I want to start, but then I have a better idea. "Can you drop us next door at The Scoop?"

"If it's all right with your mother."

I can't scramble into the car fast enough. "Let's go!"

Dorit raises her eyebrows.

"It's an ice cream shop. You'll love it."

When Dad lets us in, Mom's not far behind. "Stay in back and keep your seat belts on. And don't leave The Scoop until Dad comes for you." She turns. "Martin, make sure you can see them—no wandering."

Dorit's face turns into one huge question mark. She must think our family is nuts.

Her legs make a *put-put-put* noise as we slide in across the warm vinyl seats. "Excuse me!" she says, and we both crack up. That totally cuts the tension.

I crank down the back window until the wind whips our hair. "Sit up," I say. "Since it's your first time here, I'll give you the official Melanie Adler Tour of Ashford."

Dad turns onto Ashford Avenue, the main drag. "See that building with the big windows over there?" I say. "That's the Jewish community center—you know, the JCC. I took ballet there a gazillion years ago when I was little." I point to the stop sign across the street. "Jon crashed his bike here last summer and got twelve stitches." We pass a brick structure with a *Save Soviet Jews* sign in front. "That's Temple Menorah," I say, "our synagogue. Maybe I'll see you there some Saturday."

"I wish. We go to services at Hillel House, the Jewish student organization at the university. Ooh, is that a record store?"

"Yeah, Record City—$3.99 albums."

At a building with painted windows, I chuckle. "My old nursery school. My mom had to drag me in 'cause I'd cry. I had trouble with goodbyes."

Dad parks at Buck's Hardware Store and dumps a pocketful of change into my hands. "Meet me back here when you're through. And you know," he says with a weary look, "don't wander off."

"This is cool," says Dorit as we enter The Scoop next door. The speakers blare Radio WLAK. Fluorescent posters hang from the walls. I smile; I knew she'd love it.

After we each order a mini scoop, we climb onto lime-green stools at the front window. Cars streak past on the busy street.

"So you've always lived here, on these few blocks?" Dorit asks. "Ever since you were born?" When she rattles off the places her family has lived— Israel, England, Canada—I feel like a little kid who's never been anywhere.

"This . . . this is my home." Until now, I've never felt embarrassed about living here my whole life.

Dorit licks ice cream off the side of her cone. "Wow," she says. "I don't like leaving friends behind; that part's hard. But living all over makes you see things differently than only staying in one town. I know kids our age who speak, like, three different languages, and—" She stops for a second. "I . . . I don't mean that in a snobby way or anything . . ."

I crunch through my cone and wipe my mouth with a napkin. I've suddenly turned into the most boring person on Earth. "I've been to lots of places on vacation," I say, remembering riding on It's a Small World at Disneyland and crawling up the steep San Francisco hills in cable cars. All before the accident. I don't tell her that ever since then, we don't go anywhere. Last summer our car was all packed for Door County, this cool place in Wisconsin with beaches and little shops, and right before we were supposed to leave, Mom said she couldn't go. I could tell she felt horrible about it, but there was no way anyone could change her mind.

"I know some people think the Midwest is super dull," I continue, "but Ashford is only fifteen minutes from the city, and we have museums and the university—"

"That's why we moved here. My father's going to be a professor there. He thinks it's finally time to settle down."

The blowing of the air conditioner sends a dull hum throughout The Scoop. I picture our family moving every few years, leaving my pink-and-green bedroom and the lilac bushes I smell every spring on my way to catch the school bus. I feel bad for someone like Dorit who doesn't have one special place to call home. Maybe she'll think that makes me uninteresting, but I like being from Ashford. Someday—after college, after I travel the world, when I'm writing cookbooks or I'm a chef running my own restaurant—maybe I'll come back and live here.

A knock on the window startles me.

"Ready to go," mouths Dad, holding two sheets of pegboard the length of his body. Outside, Mr. Buckman slides the boards into the trunk and helps to fasten the rope holding the trunk closed. "How's Barb doing?" he asks Dad. "She all healed up from the last surgery?"

"Yeah, this one wasn't too bad. The plastic surgeon thinks she may be done for a while." Dad gives one final tug to the knot. "Hard to believe we're still dealing with that accident."

The whole way home, the boards hang from the trunk and jiggle whenever we hit a bump. After we pull into the driveway, Dad tells me, "Go call your brother out here to put these boards in the garage. I'll start the grill for dinner."

Dorit jumps out of the car and grabs one end of a long pegboard. "That's okay," she tells him. "We can do it."

The unfinished edges of wood scrape against my hands as I shimmy the other end of the board from the trunk. Dorit tightens her lips as we hoist them up, leaning each one in the same direction against the garage wall.

"I am woman, hear me roar!" says Dorit, dusting off her hands with a clap.

"Girl power!" I flex my arms.

Inside, Jon's stereo throbs—he keeps playing an album by some new singer named Bruce Springsteen who mumbles every word. Mom pulls a pot out of the kitchen cabinet with a clatter. But when we reach the basement, the noises upstairs fade away.

"Wow!" says Dorit. "This place is so cool. It's like having our own apartment." She plops down on one of the sofas I made up with sheets and blankets. "You've even got a TV down here!"

"Yeah. It's old, and black and white, but it still works. And look at this stereo—my dad built the speakers himself. The best part is that nobody else uses this room. Jon hates it down here 'cause he thinks it's too cold. I'd put on five sweaters to have it all to myself."

Dorit drops onto the oval rug and tugs the zipper on her bag. It's almost empty. When Vicky sleeps over, she brings one suitcase for her makeup alone.

"I like to read before I fall asleep," she says, setting a thick paperback on the table. It's at least three hundred pages long and looks like something from Jon's advanced English class. Her balled-up pajamas hit the sofa with a bounce, while her cuffed blue jeans and sweatshirt peek out from a side pocket.

"You have a lot of albums." She thumbs through my pile of records. "Stevie Wonder . . . John Denver . . . ooh, Elton John. I love this! Can you play it? Mine are still in storage."

I pull it out of its jacket and drop the disc onto the turntable. Once the first piano notes of "Rocket Man" float through the speakers, Dorit sings along, unembarrassed. Her voice is pretty—soft and breathy. "What's the matter?" she asks, turning down the volume. "Don't you like to sing?"

"Well, yeah, but not in front of anyone."

"But it's such an amazing song. It's about this guy who's an astronaut and how sad he feels when he's so far from his family. Like he's just this regular guy, but everyone thinks he's a hero." She smiles at me. "I'm not going to make fun of your voice or anything."

"Okay." I turn the music back up. "Here goes!"

This time I join her as she sings. At the end, we hold the last note together.

She grabs my arm. "You have a great voice!"

"You really think so?" I feel a flush of pride; no one's ever complimented my singing before. Possibly because I never sing in front of others.

I'm still beaming when Mom calls us for dinner.

"Vicky called while you were out," Mom says, piling steaming corn on a plate. "I don't know what she wanted; it seemed like *she* wasn't sure. There was all sorts of laughing in the background."

My stomach tightens. Vicky and the Shimmers gathered around the telephone—ugh. "She's at Jan Rosen's. They were probably bored." Maybe Vicky wasn't calling to talk—they might've been pulling something on me. I don't think Vicky would embarrass me just to look cool, but I'm not sure.

Dad carries in a platter of barbecued chicken, smelling sweet and smoky. "I heated the charcoal to perfection. Wait till you taste the chicken. And that's Melanie's homemade barbecue sauce."

"My dad's a chemist," I explain. "Sometimes he thinks he's still in his lab when he's actually in the kitchen."

Dorit waits until everyone else serves themselves before she takes food, but soon we check out each other's plates piled high with chicken, corn, salad, rolls, and baked potatoes.

"Guess we're hungry," I giggle.

"Guess you're a couple of cows," says Jon, who's busy inhaling his dinner. He lets out a major burp.

"Guess he's gross," I whisper to Dorit. We snicker.

"You don't need all that starch," Mom scolds, giving Dad's plate the once-over. "Two rolls *and* a huge potato—take it easy."

"Barb, did you see how little I ate for lunch today?"

At least he has the sense to whisper, but I want to crawl under the table. Just because he's stocky doesn't mean he's about to drop over from a heart attack— unless you think disaster's around every corner. I wish we could go through one meal like other families.

"*Skeeeuze me!*" Jon stands up and scratches his curly head of hair. "I heard Radio Moscow on my shortwave radio last night. I want to see if I can find it again." When Dad nods, he's gone. Dorit and I are finished eating too.

"Thanks for dinner," says Dorit. "It was delicious." She pops up like she can sense the awkwardness and wants to get out of the way. After she rinses her plate in the sink, she waves me toward the basement door. "C'mon, Mel. Let's go." She must see how much I want to get out of here.

"You'll need extra blankets; it's freezing down there," Mom says before we reach the bottom of the steps.

"Don't worry," says Dorit. "I'm used to it. When we lived in England, our apartment had this puny kerosene heater, so we wore sweaters all the time."

I shoot Mom a look. Immediately, I feel guilty; the basement *is* cold.

Downstairs, we sing the entire Elton John album. When a fast song comes on, Dorit turns up the volume.

"Do you like to dance?" I ask.

"Ugh, I stink. I try to copy other people, but my hips are frozen in place!"

"You should come to the JCC for Tweens' Night Out. Their jukebox plays the Top Forty songs on Thursday nights, and all the junior high kids from Ashford and Highland Hills go. Shari and Marla are amazing dancers."

"You are totally starstruck when those airheads are around." She frowns.

"I am not! I only said they're good dancers—"

"Oh, so you want to see some good dancing?" She blasts the volume. "Watch this!" She leans forward and rocks from one foot to the other, hips swaying, head bobbing, feet pounding to the beat of the music.

"Hey, Jon, you wanna see Dorit dance?" I yell,

looking past her. Dorit freezes and whips her head around.

"Gotcha!" I sing out.

"I'm gonna get you!" Dorit says, making a fierce face. She grabs a pillow and throws it, missing me, but she knocks a baby picture of Jon off our paneled wall.

We're doubled over, howling with laughter.

"Everything all right?" Mom calls from upstairs. I'm so out of breath I can barely croak out an answer.

Later, after we're in our pajamas, I turn off the lights and flip on the TV. Some boring show about gorillas.

"Melanie?" It's Mom again. This time she creeps down with a flashlight. "I didn't hear anything. Are you okay?"

"Just getting ready for bed." I don't even turn to look at her. I want her to leave us alone.

I fiddle with the antenna on top of the TV so the picture will stop jumping.

Dorit watches Mom go back upstairs. "Is everything okay?"

My heart pounds as I wiggle the knob, first left and then right, trying to bring the gorillas into focus. "Yeah. She just . . ." I trail off. I haven't had to explain any of this stuff—Mom, the accident, the cloud of fear that hangs over our house every second—in so long.

41

Eventually I turn from the TV and scrunch down next to her on the rug. "She was in an accident. I mean, we all were."

"I heard your dad talking to Mr. Buckman at the hardware store. And I . . . I noticed the scars on her face."

I hug my knees close. "It happened two years ago, on the drive to New York to visit my grandparents."

Dorit sits still and watches me talk.

"We were somewhere in Michigan when the sky turned freaky black and it started raining really hard. It sounded like someone dumping gravel over the roof of our car. All of a sudden, I felt a huge crash, and our car started spinning."

I swallow hard while a gorilla thunders through the jungle on the TV.

"I heard glass shattering and my mom moan. And when she turned around, I fainted."

"That's horrible," Dorit whispers.

"When I woke up in the backseat, I asked Jon, 'Am I dreaming?' and he answered, 'No, this is real.' I couldn't even remember where we'd been driving."

I grab a blanket off the sofa and wrap it around my shoulders. "As they wheeled Mom and me into the ambulance, I kept saying, 'Don't worry, you'll be all right,' but I think I was trying to convince myself more than her."

My voice catches, and I blink my stinging eyes. I didn't expect talking about it to be so hard.

"You don't have to tell me more," says Dorit, pulling at a thread on her pajamas. After a minute she asks, "Your mom . . . she's okay now, right?"

"She made us dinner tonight, remember?" We both force a laugh.

"I didn't mean to make you upset."

Dorit looks so earnest that I don't know how to answer. "It's okay. She's feeling a lot better, only . . . she still thinks about it a lot."

"I noticed how she made sure we buckled our seat belts before we left for The Scoop."

"She was trying to hold back because you've never been here before," I say, "but she's scared of everything. You should see the way she jumps whenever the doorbell rings, and how she paces the house until we're all home from work and school. She once told me that when she woke up in her hospital bed after the accident, none of the doctors or nurses could even tell her if we were alive or not. She said she'll never forget that feeling—it must've been so scary."

Dorit pulls apart a balled-up tissue. "This might sound strange, but I think I know how you feel. I've never told anyone this before . . . My father fought in the Six-Day War in Israel when I was only six." Her voice sounds shaky. "I didn't get what was happening back then, but now I know how horrible it must've been. He told me how one night he felt a huge explosion, and when he looked around, his best friend was lying on the ground."

The tissue sits in shreds in her lap. The blue glow of the television casts shadows across the room.

"My dad was in shock. At first, he didn't realize his own leg was injured. He still thinks about it. He won't let our family go anyplace crowded, and he goes nuts when people walk behind him and he can't see what's going on. Sometimes he's really quiet and sad."

I swipe at the tears pooling in my eyes. When Mom held me tight the day I was late coming home from school, I was sure there wasn't another kid in the world who understood what it's like to live in a house full of fear. I can't believe Dorit gets this. And she's here, sleeping over. And becoming my friend.

"Promise you won't tell anyone about my father, okay?" Dorit sighs. "We're here now, in a new place, and maybe things will be better."

"I swear."

When I get up to turn off the TV, an enormous gorilla appears on the screen, scratching his butt. We laugh so hard that Dorit can't stop coughing.

"Can you grab my puffer?" She motions to her

overnight bag. I toss her the small metal canister, and she inhales a burst of medicine. "That's better," she says after a few deep breaths.

"Good thing the gorilla showed up," I say. "Otherwise we'd be crying ourselves to sleep tonight." We erupt into another round of giggles.

Later, after we've crawled under our blankets and Dorit's breathing has turned soft and steady, I start working on the needlepoint peace sign I've been stitching. My mind replays everything we talked about.

There are so many things I didn't say—like how I wanted to punch this kid in the nose for staring at Mom's scars one time when we were waiting at the dentist's office. Or how different I feel from every other kid.

But somehow, I think she'd understand.

Chapter 4

MONDAY MORNING, I SLIP ON MY FAVORITE PAIR of worn-in Levi's and the T-shirt I studded with rhinestones from my craft corner. I packed my book bag last night and left it by the front door so I wouldn't have to turn my messy bedroom upside down to find it today. It's so early I'll bet the school bus hasn't even started its route yet. I can't remember the last time I felt so excited to get to school. I have a new friend, and she's not like anyone I've ever met.

Jon's at the kitchen table, muttering something about President Nixon being a liar, his face buried deep in the newspaper.

"Watergate, Watergate! That's all you ever talk about," I say as I drop a slice of bread into the toaster.

"Shh! Keep it down. Mom's still in bed. Didn't you hear her pacing last night?" Jon's said so much in a few words. When she's up all night, the next day ends up being a dark one. Seeing her like that makes me sad too, like I'm a balloon someone's poked a hole through.

"How long have you been up?" I ask him, trying to shake it off. "Since the paper got delivered?"

"What if I have?" He straightens his gold aviator glasses. "It's not my fault high school has a late start today. It gives me more time to catch up on the news."

The front page of the *Tribune* rattles in his hands with the headline "Watergate Sinks Top Aides."

"Every other kid reads the comics or maybe the sports page, you know." I unscrew the top of the jar of strawberry jam and spread a thick layer on my toast until it glistens. On the back of the news section there's an ad for the cassette tape player I want.

Jon shrugs. "That's their loss."

Last night, our whole family watched President Nixon's boring speech together. At least I didn't miss anything good; Sunday nights have the worst TV shows of all: *The Wonderful World of Disney*, which lately is about sheep or raccoons, or *M*A*S*H*, which is supposed to be a comedy but is about doctors in a war zone, and Mom refuses to watch it because of the blood and operations.

Anyway, everyone's making a big deal about President Nixon in the news, but all he announced was that a bunch of his top advisors are resigning.

Even though I heard every dull word of his speech, I had no idea what he was talking about until Dad explained it. He said that last year when President Nixon ran for reelection, burglars broke into the office of the Democrats—the ones running against President Nixon—at the Watergate Hotel. I thought hotels just had rooms and lobbies and maybe swimming pools, but this one is huge and has offices in it too. When police came to investigate the burglary, they found all sorts of hidden microphones and recorders. Somebody had been spying on the Democrats to learn their secrets. Turns out, President Nixon's advisors were in on the spying. Some even planned it!

"They spied? Isn't that against the law?"

Dad nodded. "It sure is. You can't meddle in an election. What if we couldn't vote fairly for our leaders?" He looked all serious when he said it, and now, at least, I'm starting to understand the big fuss.

Dad and Jon watched President Nixon like detectives, trying to find holes in his story. Jon says the big question is whether President Nixon knew about the break-in, but I already know what he thinks.

Before I head for the front door, I tiptoe down the hall and stand outside Mom's room. Her clock radio hums the news, and she's lying next to a twisted mound of blankets.

"Mommy, are you okay?" I whisper, moving closer to her bed.

She reaches up and pulls me down into a hug. "Come here." My cheek rests on her warm pillow. The traffic report drones on: backups, a fender bender, a disabled vehicle in the right lane . . . Maybe she shouldn't listen to news of car accidents first thing in the morning.

"I've been thinking about the weather warming up now," she says, fingering a strand of my hair. "You need to stay alert *all the time*. People drive like maniacs in summer. And all kinds of dangerous people come out. I don't want you walking alone."

Whenever she says, *I've been thinking* . . . it really means she stayed up all night imagining horrible things that could happen. For most people, summer means sunshine and picnics and bike rides. For her it means cars driving too fast, people lurking in parks, and swimming pool water way over my head.

I hug her hard. "I'm always careful," I say. "You don't have to worry, okay?" Every time I force myself to stay all cheery and calm, reassuring her about another one of her worries, it's like someone's placing a heavy rock on top of me. *One more . . . one more.* It's not like we're going to get to the end of her list and she'll run out of things to worry about. The pile of rocks keeps pushing down.

The whole way to the bus stop, I'm spooked, even

as the sun warms my face, even as a robin lands on our maple tree and tweets a song. I hate that Mom makes me scared of normal things like riding the bus to school every morning and walking home with Vicky every afternoon. We live close enough that I could walk in the mornings too, but the way Vicky oversleeps, I'd be walking by myself most days, and that's impossible for Mom to handle.

When I reach the clump of lilac bushes past our house, I can almost hear her voice in my head, telling me to scoot away—telling me that someone might be hiding behind there and could jump out at any second. Instead, I stop and take my sweet time inhaling the scent of the flowers. I'm not letting her scare me about every little thing I do.

Dorit's not in the cafeteria at lunch. Instead, Vicky sneaks up behind me. "Here I am!" She's wearing striped bell-bottoms I've never seen before, and she fans open the pages of a worn paperback. "Look what I borrowed from Jan," she says. "*Go Ask Alice.* I already started it. It's so *heavy.* You can read it when I'm done."

"Maybe." That's all Mom needs to see—the diary of a girl my age who starts using drugs and runs away from home. Forget about walking alone—she'd never let me leave the house again.

The cluster of orange and olive-green tables in the center of the cafeteria looks like someone's living room. The Shimmers stretch out on their chairs, pass food back and forth, and chatter like it's a Saturday night. Jerry grabs something from this redheaded girl, Julie. She's half his height, and whenever she dodges around him, he practically trips over his big feet.

"Let me see my true feelings!" he yells. She's holding one of those new mood rings with a stone that changes colors depending on how you feel when you're wearing it. If I put it on now, it would turn green for jealousy. None of the Shimmers have moms who stay up all night picturing all the horrible things that could happen.

"Hey, space case, come and sit down." Vicky's lunch is spread out at the table she saved for us.

"Oh, sorry," I say. "How was your sleepover?" I fiddle with the ends of my lunch bag. It's weird that she wants to sit here with me instead of over there, especially since she spent practically the whole weekend with the Shimmers.

"The sleepover? Oh, it was super fun." Vicky puts a lilt in her voice, but the way she bites into her apple, instead of gushing about how they gossiped and played Spoons all night, makes me skeptical.

"Really?" I say. "You don't sound so excited."

"No, it was awesome." Vicky flips her hair like she doesn't want me to see how uncomfortable she is. "It's just, they've known each other since they were little, like us. I didn't get all their private jokes." She pulls the stem out of her apple. "Anyway, I'm sorry I canceled on you. Next time, we'll bake the castle cake you've been wanting to try—if you trust me not to mess it up."

When she puts her arm around me, a warm feeling grows in my chest. The old Vicky shows up when I least expect it. Maybe I was wrong; maybe she's not a Shimmer yet.

"What'd you do, anyway?" she asks. "You weren't stuck watching *The Partridge Family* with your parents again, were you?"

"Ha ha—I don't watch that baby show anymore," I say. When Dorit shows up in line, paying for a carton of milk, I wave wildly. "Actually, she slept over." Dorit smiles, but on her way over to us, she stumbles on a book some Shimmer left on the floor. When everyone at their tables cracks up, something inside me stings. She might not care what they think, but *I* do.

"Dorit?" The look that grows on Vicky's face is one I hardly ever see, like an open safety pin is poking inside her shirt but she's trying to act like it's not.

The last time I remember it happening was when Josh Weber, an eighth grader, told me I looked cute in my new outfit. When he said it, I felt myself turning red hot, and I looked away, but inside, I felt all sparkly. I couldn't wait to tell Vicky. Only when I did, as we changed into gym suits in the locker room, she said, "Big deal. Boys tell me that all the time." And there was that look on her face.

"You two are friends?" Vicky hoists her feet up on the open chair next to me. "I thought you were just showing her around."

I thought so too.

I don't say that something huge happened Saturday night, that Dorit understands my family more than anyone I've ever met. And that, even though she's lived in so many places and I haven't, her life feels so much like mine.

"It wasn't a big deal. Just a sleepover." It feels important to keep the details to myself. I shouldn't have to—I mean, Vicky has other friends besides me. But her face looks awfully jealous. "Besides, you were busy trying on Jan's entire closet."

"You like these?" Vicky models the bell-bottoms. "She said I can keep them as long as I want."

"Keep what?" Dorit looks down at Vicky's feet resting on the open chair.

"Oh, nothing," says Vicky. She eyes Dorit in a *how-long-are-you-gonna-stand-here* way. Two sets of eyes land on me to see what I'm going to do next. I have a weird feeling it won't be the last time this happens.

"I'll find you a chair," I say. "There's plenty of room." When Vicky coughs, I'm not sure if it's real or a message that she doesn't want Dorit to sit with us. Some other kid might back off, but Dorit doesn't care; she's smiling so big she's practically stretching her freckles.

"Never mind," she says. "I have news!" She grabs my arm before I'm done dragging another chair over. "You'll never guess what!"

"Um . . . you finished our entire math book last night? Wait, *that's* not news."

"Very funny." She plops her folders down. "My parents found a house over the weekend. We're moving in two weeks when school is over."

"Are you kidding? That was really fast!"

She digs into her lunch bag. "I know! And it's the one on Mulberry your mom told us about."

"That's only a few blocks from my house. You'll be right in the neighborhood." My head spins with summer possibilities.

"You'll have to come over and help me set up my new room," Dorit says. "My *own* room—no more sharing with my brothers. And I need another Ashford

Tour." She unwraps a foil mound and bites into a sandwich filled with beige spread and sprouts. "I think we're here for good!"

She sounds super happy for someone who, two days ago, told me that moving around makes you a more interesting person.

A Rip Van Winkle look settles on Vicky's face, like she's slept through something big, as she watches Dorit and me talk. I try to pull her into the conversation. "Isn't that cool? Dorit's moving right near us."

But that face—the cover-up—*bam!* It's back on Vicky in a flash. "Why would you want to live in our neighborhood?" She says it like something stinks. "All the cute guys live in Highland Hills."

Dorit's ears turn pink before she smooths her ponytail over them. "Oh, shoot! I forgot to ask my parents for pictures of all the boys in the neighborhood before they bought the house." Her voice is full of needles.

Vicky tilts her head like she's not sure what Dorit said, but after a moment she gets it. "Suit yourself," she says with a sniff.

"Wait until you see the Ashford pool," I say to Dorit, trying to break the tension. "Do you have a bike?"

"Not yet. I'm working on my parents, but my mom says if I babysit I can buy one myself."

"Yeah, the Ashford pool is a blast." Vicky pulls her chair close to me. "I'll give you that. We'd be there every day, Mel, if I wasn't going to stay with my cousins in California. *And* if your mom would finally let you go there alone instead of sitting at the edge of the pool to make sure you don't drown."

She makes these comments all the time, mostly as jokes. Sometimes they keep me from getting too wrapped up in Mom's worries. But sitting here with Dorit, who doesn't just *get* it but lives with it like I do, I feel something snap inside me.

"That's not funny, Vicky. You know she can't help it." I'm surprised by how much my voice shakes. Vicky should've seen how scared Mom was this morning.

Dorit pushes away her lunch, and her eyes harden on Vicky. "You have a lot to learn about your *best friend*."

"Whoa! You two need to cool it," says Vicky. To me, she adds, "My jokes never used to bother you." She flashes me an accusing look, and something shifts in the tiniest way—I don't rush to try to make her feel better.

"Well, maybe they do now," I say. And I mean it.

Chapter 5

THE LAST FEW WEEKS OF SCHOOL ARE LIKE THE final miles of a long car trip. You know you're close, but all the tricks you've used to make it this far stop working because you can see the end and you're sick of waiting.

"Can you stop by tomorrow after dinner to say goodbye?" Vicky asks me on our way outside on the second-to-last day of school.

We pass a teacher on a stepladder taking psychedelic art projects off the wall. I nod. "How long are you going to be gone?"

"Six glorious weeks away from this dump of doom." She links her arm through mine. "You know I don't mean *you*, right? You're the only thing I'm gonna miss here."

"You never stayed this long before."

"This time I pleaded." She wrinkles her nose. "There are only so many times I can splash around the Ashford pool and ride my bike to the Kwik-Mart for slushies. My aunt Helene is great at talking my mom into things."

Swimming and riding our bikes are things I wait for all year, what I dream about on snowy days. But it's not enough for her anymore. Does that mean I'm not enough either?

The next day, after the final bell rings and the school year is officially over, Shari and Marla and Jan surround Vicky in a hug by the flagpole. Scores of kids stream past us, whooping and hollering. Vicky's arm reaches back, and she pulls me in until I'm face-to-face, shoulder-to-shoulder with the group—cherry lip gloss, peppermint gum, and Love's Baby Soft perfume intermingling. They giggle and teeter against one another until someone leans too hard and we scramble to keep from falling over.

"See you in August!" Vicky tells the Shimmers with a wave. As we inch through the crowd, I hear Shari ask, "Who was that kid with Vicky?"

I swallow the lump in my throat. I am invisible.

We don't talk much on the way home. I can't tell if Vicky heard Shari or not, and I'm too humiliated to bring it up.

After dinner that night, while Mom's washing the dishes, I stay casual as if I'm about to brush my teeth and put on pajamas. Jon grabs his Mad Libs book and asks us to call out nouns and adjectives. Mom plays along, looking relaxed, so I figure I'm safe. "I'm going to Vicky's to say goodbye," I announce. "She's leaving for California tomorrow."

A plate slips from Mom's soapy hands and smacks against the counter. "Who's taking you?"

"No one. She lives a whole four blocks away." I squeeze my fists behind my back, reminding myself not to get angry.

"You're walking there alone? Martin, did you hear?"

"Hmm?" Dad peeks out from the newspaper.

"She wants to walk to Vicky's house *now*."

Dad gives me a tired, *don't-make-a-scene* look.

"Let Mom take you," Jon pipes up. "What's the big deal? You're gonna be there for, like, five minutes."

You'd think I'd said, "I'm going to stand in the middle of the highway now," the way everyone jumps on me. Maybe Dorit goes through this every time she tries to leave her house too.

"I want to stay for a while," I say, trying not to let them hear my voice choke. "I'm not going to see her all summer."

Mom twists a checkered dish towel around her hands, and all I can do is slip on my sandals and surrender.

The drive takes less than a minute. Mom parks at the curb in front of Vicky's house. "I'll wait right here."

In case I wasn't sure.

Vicky meets me outside. She's holding her dog, Toby, on a leash.

"I thought you'd be packing," I say.

Toby scampers to me, tail wagging, sniffing me all over. "Joel forgot to walk him," she tells me, rolling her eyes. "Come with me."

Mom's car sits like a guard station. "I can't. She thinks I'm going to get kidnapped."

Vicky loosens her grip and lets Toby wander the front yard. "Ooh, you didn't like it when *I* made a joke."

"Yeah, I guess it hit me wrong."

Toby sniffs a row of bushes and picks one to pee on. "Or you didn't want me to say it in front of Dorit," she says, "now that you two are so tight."

"Can we forget about that? I came to say goodbye to *you*." I swat at the mosquitoes flying around my head.

Vicky ignores my attempt to change the subject. "I don't get it—you two are so different."

I don't know why she thinks that. Dorit and I feel alike in all the important ways. We understand the things that no one else gets about us.

Toby wanders back, rubbing his head against my arm until I scratch his ears. "I don't get why you dislike her so much," I say. "She's smart. And funny. And she has so many cool stories from living all over the world." It seems like the more I say, the more annoyed the look on Vicky's face becomes. I wish we weren't doing this right before she leaves.

"Well, you're never gonna become a Shimmer by being friends with her. She's a weirdo; she wears the same baggy jeans every day, and she always walks around all serious like the world's about to end."

I don't know if she's telling me the truth or if she's just jealous that Dorit and I are becoming friends. It sounds more like what she *wants* me to think about Dorit.

She picks a bug off of Toby's ear. "This summer you should be riding your bike to the pool every morning and joining the Ashford Splashers. All the Shimmers compete, and they'd get to know you that way. Plus you're a fast swimmer."

"Oh, sure—I'll tell my mom to sign me right up. She'll be all for it."

When Mom notices us looking at her, she leans over and rolls down the passenger window. "Is something the matter?"

I shoot Vicky a knowing look. My neck itches from a fresh mosquito bite. "Just saying goodbye." I hug Vicky, long and hard. "Have a good summer," I say.

I can't resist adding, "And when you get back, maybe you can give Dorit a chance. You don't even know her."

"No, but I know *you*."

I wonder if that's still true.

★ ★ ★

Early the next morning, WLAK pulses from my radio. Elton John. Stevie Wonder. John Denver. Last summer their songs became as much a part of me as the freckles on my sunburned shoulders.

I stuff a bottle of baby oil, a towel, and my radio into a beach bag and jump on my bike.

Mom appears outside in her droopy bathrobe. "Where are you going?"

"Didn't I tell you yesterday?" I lie. "I'm going to Dorit's new house to help her unpack." I hide my swimsuit strap under my sleeve. She doesn't need to know about our pool plans yet.

"How about you invite her here instead? Her mother probably has a mess on her hands with all those boxes."

"*No.* I'm going." It's just the two of us; Dad's at work, and Jon's still asleep. No one can interfere and try to keep me here. I'm not staying home all summer.

I lay my bike on the ground next to the curb and dig a slip of paper out of my shorts pocket. "Here's her address." I hand it to her. "It's on Mulberry, right in the neighborhood."

Mom's face scrunches into a foreboding frown as she takes a step back toward the house. "I'll wake Jon to go with you."

"No! I don't need Jon to take me there like I'm a baby." I'm trying to stay strong and sure of myself, but it feels more like I'm being mean. I climb back on my bicycle. "I'll be careful. Would you stop worrying?" I pound my feet onto the pedals.

"Call me as soon as you get there," she yells.

"I'm only going four blocks away; nothing's going to happen to me!" I holler back, into the wind.

The ride to Dorit's house is all downhill, and aside from the beach bag across my chest, nothing holds me down.

Freedom.

The breeze shoots through my hair, flapping it in all directions, and I fly for all four blocks. I only slow down when I reach Dorit's gravel driveway.

Her house looks nothing like ours. Around here, most are made of brick and look like they came from the same fifteen-year-old mold. Dad says Dorit's is one of the original frame houses from back when Ashford was all farmland.

"Come in," says Mrs. Shoshani, with a screech of

the door. "How do you think? We worked all day yesterday, but still it's such a balagan—a big mess."

"It's really nice," I say. "I like the wood floors and that big window." Their worn-out furniture looks as if it's moved all over with them from place to place. And books—piles and piles everywhere: university books that must belong to Dorit's father, but also novels and volumes on art, most of them in Hebrew.

"Is your phone connected yet? I . . . I need to call home for a second."

Mrs. Shoshani points me toward the kitchen, where a yellow phone hangs on the wall. I give Mom the quickest "I made it here" I can muster without sounding obnoxious, then untangle the coiled-up phone cord before I hang up the receiver. The house is quiet except for the sound of Mrs. Shoshani pushing boxes around on the wood floor. If Dorit hadn't told me about her father, I wonder if I'd be able to guess that something's wrong in her family. I wonder if people can guess when they first walk into *our* house.

Dorit's little brothers sit perched at the kitchen table, eating cucumber slices and crusty bread slathered in butter.

"Hi, guys! How's it going?"

"We have a new house!" says Benny, his little hand grasping mine. "And Natan and I have a new bedroom."

Dorit peeks out of the bathroom, her hair wrapped in a towel. "I'll be ready in a minute. Go look at my room!"

Making my way down the hall, I see that clothes are already hanging in closets and bins of toys sit stacked in the boys' room, but a small black-and-white television still lies in a box in the corner, its cord wrapped in a ball.

When Dorit emerges, dressed in a fresh tank top and shorts, I tap the box with my toe. "At our house that TV would've been the first thing that got unpacked. Jon has plans to watch the Watergate hearings all day. They're on for hours, on every channel. I don't get why the Senate can't start their investigation after *The Price Is Right.*"

"What's *The Price Is Right?*" she asks, pulling her damp hair through a rubber band.

"Never mind."

"Okay, guys." Dorit gives Benny and Natan a push into the hall. "See you later." They fire back with a symphony of pounding on the closed door.

"Here's the best part." She clicks the lock. "Mwahaha!"

It takes time to arrange and rearrange, but we cram every one of her books—thick novels and history collections—into the built-in shelves next to her bed. My head would explode if I tried reading half the stuff she likes. Personally, I prefer to stick with Judy Blume.

Dorit fingers a thick rubber-banded packet of envelopes, looking for a place to stash them.

"What's that?" I ask.

"Letters. From Canada . . . England . . . from all my friends. At least I think we're still friends."

Maybe she *is* happy to settle down in one place.

"Can you help me hang these posters? I buy them at art museums whenever we visit a new city." Her arms cradle a pile of cardboard tubes. I dig through one of the boxes until I find a roll of tape, then pull a folding chair over to the wall.

"That looks awesome," I say once the last one is up. "Who's that by, again?"

"Matisse. And those are by Monet, Renoir, and Picasso." Their names roll off her tongue as easily as the list of top ten songs rolls off mine.

After a lull, the door pounding starts again. "Let us in! Let us in!" Dorit's brothers chant. When she pulls the door open, they fall inside and burst into giggles.

"Stop bugging us," she says. "Go find something else to do."

I mouth "Pool" to her, and she nods as they scamper off.

"Grab my swimsuit and that towel," she says, following her brothers. "And stick them inside your bag so they can't see."

In the kitchen, Dorit pours orange juice into two tall, mismatched glasses and sets them in front of the boys. "Where's Ema?" she asks.

They shrug.

"*Ee-mah!*" I can't understand the cascade of Hebrew that follows until Benny and Natan start chanting, "We want to swim too! We want to swim too!" and march into the living room.

Mrs. Shoshani sits crouched on the floor in sandals and jeans. She pushes strands of loose hair out of her face as she sets up shelves with bricks and boards.

"Yalla, chamudah! Go to the pool before I change my mind," she says to Dorit. "They can play outside."

"Really?"

"Wait," I say. "I . . . I need to call my mom first and ask her—"

"Give me your number and I can call. I have questions for her anyway; the boys need a new doctor . . ."

Ugh. It shouldn't be a big deal. I'm going to the pool with Dorit, and Mrs. Shoshani's calling Mom to let her know. But it's a huge deal.

"Is it okay that we're going?" Dorit whispers. "I heard Vicky's joke at lunch."

"My mom will probably freak out. She might even show up at the pool."

"Hold on a minute," says Dorit, and then she says a whole long thing to her mom in Hebrew.

Mrs. Shoshani pushes herself up off the floor and gives me a knowing smile—sad, but not like she feels sorry for me. "I will take care with your mother," she says. "It will be okay."

"What did you say to her?" I whisper to Dorit.

Dorit pulls me toward their front door. "I told her your mom worries like my abba does sometimes. She gets it."

I can't believe how much better I suddenly feel. No one's trying to make a joke about our situation, and I don't have to come up with flimsy excuses about why I can't go to the pool. It doesn't mean everything's okay with Mom, or even normal, but the Shoshanis understand.

"Now we have to figure out how to get there," Dorit says, like maybe her mom will stop building her bookshelves and give us a ride.

Mrs. Shoshani comes to the door and kisses Dorit's head. "You're a smart girl. You'll figure it out. Besides, Abba took the car to the university." She swipes her rag across the dusty board she's holding. "Yalla, boys! We have our own yard now." She gives us our chance to slip out front while she shoos the boys to the patio.

"I'll bet the pool isn't so close, is it?" Dorit asks as we stand on her front porch. Sweat beads on her forehead.

"It's at least a half-hour walk." I eye my bike. "But . . . have you ever been bucked before?"

"Once you tell me what it means, I'll tell you if I have," Dorit answers with a chuckle.

"Hop on." I mount the bike and inch forward to make room on the seat. "I'll show you."

We zigzag down the streets and sidewalks, drenched in sweat, and cracking up.

"You are a wild driver!" says Dorit at the pool entrance. "You almost rode us into the ditch! And look at the scratch on my leg from that rosebush you plowed into!"

"It's not my fault. You think it's easy steering two people on this hunk of metal? Next time, you can steer the whole way here."

"If there *is* a next time. We still have to make it home alive first."

We display our bare feet on an overturned wire basket for the humiliating "foot check" by one of the lifeguards, and Dorit whispers, "What do they think they're going to find?!" Finally, we're allowed to plunge into the deep end. Cool water. Laughter. Sun. Heaven.

When I'm here with Vicky, she's always daring me to try flips and dives we're not really supposed to do in this pool. Today, Dorit and I race each other. We have a contest to see who can make the biggest splash. And we swim to the bottom of the deep end to see who can grab rubber rings first.

The day is perfect.

Until Shari and Marla show up. And Jerry, and Jan, and every other Shimmer from our grade. They're wearing *Ashford Splashers* tank tops, and they gather by the high dive, whooping every time one of them jumps off.

I can't stop myself from watching them. If Vicky were here, we'd go up to them. Well, *she* would, and I'd follow. They might not notice me or care whether I was there or not, but I'd be with them, and . . . I don't know, maybe something would happen. Maybe one of them would talk to me. Maybe that's how it would start.

I straighten the straps on my polka-dot bathing suit, which they'd call babyish. Dorit bounces through the water, not bothered by her faded black suit or her pale skin splattered all over with freckles.

Do I really want to do this? Before I can overthink it, I hoist myself out of the pool and onto the concrete deck. The Shimmers watch as I drip my way over. I'm just going to get in line. Maybe someone will say hi.

"Hey, Miss Model Student! Why aren't you still at school?" Jerry smirks. Everyone cracks up. I turn away and jump back into the pool. It's summer vacation and they're *still* calling me that awful nickname. I will never be a Shimmer.

I'm glad my eyes are already red from the chlorine. I hope Dorit doesn't notice.

She leans over, and with the hint of a giggle, she whispers, "Jerry Finkel belongs in the kiddie pool."

I picture him flopping into the water, wearing a pair of toddler-sized Scooby Doo swim trunks. I laugh so hard I can barely tread water anymore, but it's not really the joke that makes me feel better. It's how she knew to be there for me when Jerry was so mean.

I have never met anyone as smart and funny and sure of herself as Dorit Shoshani. We have a whole summer ahead of us, and I have a new best friend.

Chapter 6

I'M SPLAYED OUT ON MOM AND DAD'S BED, phone pressed to my ear. "We broke our swimming streak," I tell Dorit. "Today would've been ten days in a row!" I say it like I'm teasing, but something in me felt sad when she canceled our plans this morning. "Where were you today, anyway? You called in such a hurry—you didn't even say where you were going."

She heaves an exasperated sigh. "My parents made us all come while they shopped at some used car lot because, last minute, my father wouldn't leave us home alone. He says our station wagon is about to die." The sound of something tumbling over fills the background, followed by giggles from her brothers. I hear stomping, followed by silence. I picture Dorit pulling the cord from her family's only phone, mounted on the kitchen wall, as far as it'll stretch so she can talk someplace quiet. "But after all that, my parents aren't even buying a car—they decided to repair ours."

"Sounds about as fun as my day," I tell her. "I

reread the diaries I kept from fifth and sixth grade."

"You must've been really bored," says Dorit.

"I didn't exactly *plan* to read them all day. They were smushed at the bottom of a box I needed to store the knitting supplies my grandparents sent."

"And fifth and sixth grade were so riveting that you couldn't put them down?" Dorit jokes.

"Very funny." It's weird, but instead of laughing, all of a sudden my voice turns wobbly, catching me completely by surprise.

"Whoa—you okay?"

"Yeah . . . I guess so."

"Doesn't sound like it," she presses.

"I'm fine." My throat's all tight, and I can barely choke out the words.

"Mel, what's wrong? I know something's bothering you. Is it 'cause I had to break our plans today?"

I pull in a shaky breath. "No, it's not that. It's those diaries—I shouldn't have read them. They reminded me of a lot of sad stuff that happened with my mom."

"Mmm," says Dorit.

"The operations, and how scared I was every time she'd go into the hospital. Then how bruised and bandaged she looked each time she'd come back home, and all the annoying grown-ups trying to talk to me about it."

73

"Yeah," says Dorit. "Those aren't exactly memories you want to keep."

I swallow hard as a tear slips from the corner of my eye. "It makes me feel guilty for all the times I've lost patience with her and said mean things. It's just that sometimes I can't help it."

"I get it," says Dorit. "I do that too."

For a while neither of us says anything. I'll bet we're both remembering times when we yelled at our parents to stop worrying so much and to leave us alone.

"Once, at the zoo in Vancouver, my abba gave the death stare to anyone who came close to me, even though they were just trying to see into the cages too. He ordered them to move back, like he worked there and they were doing something wrong. It was so embarrassing. I ended up running off to the reptile house without him. For a second it felt so cool to be left alone." Dorit's voice turns sad. "When he found me . . . man, was he angry! I *still* feel horrible for scaring him so badly. I couldn't help it, though. I had to get away."

I sigh. "Exactly."

The sounds of her brothers squabbling and a crash of something shattering carry through the phone.

"Speaking of getting away . . ." she says dryly, and we both laugh, relieved to lighten the mood.

"My abba promised I could visit the university art museum at the end of summer, right before the students come back. It'll be my reward for chasing my brothers around the car lot all afternoon today. Will you come with me?"

"The art museum?" In fifth grade, I went on a field trip to the university campus, but even our teachers knew better than to show us boring old art.

Dorit chuckles. "Okay, I'm a nerd—I know that. But I think you'd really like it. When you walk into the quiet with all these huge paintings surrounding you, it's so *peaceful*. And you can tell the artists put all their feelings into them."

"Your father will let us go there without him?"

"I haven't worked out the details yet, but he owes me big time. I caught Benny right before he was about to pee on a sports car!"

We both crack up. "If it's peaceful, I'm all in," I say, even though spending a summer day inside an art museum instead of splashing around the Ashford pool sounds completely boring. But I think of how much happier I feel after talking to her tonight, even for this little bit of time. Sometimes I can't believe how lucky I am to have a friend who understands me so well.

Weeks later, as Dorit and I bound through my front doorway after a morning of swimming, two blasts hit me at the same time: the air-conditioning, turned down nice and cool, and Mom's rendition of "If I Were a Rich Man," booming up from her new keyboard in the basement.

Dorit looks at me as if our vibrating walls are about to cave in.

"I know!" I say. "Mom played accordion when she was little, and Dad's hoping this gives her something to do besides worry every second. She only wanted a little electric piano-type thing, but my Dad figured bigger is better. This baby's a monster—crashing cymbals and cha-cha beats, and like, a whole horn section."

Eyes twinkling, Dorit hooks her arm through mine, and we kick our legs in time with the beat of the bass drum. "Are you sure there's not an actual orchestra in your basement?" she teases. When Mom ends the song with a cheesy fade-out of tambourines, we both crack up and applaud.

"Is somebody there?" I hear the keyboard power down as Mom clambers up the stairs. "I didn't even hear you come in. You didn't stay at the pool very long." Her eyes dart from me to Dorit to make sure nothing's wrong.

I shoo Dorit into the kitchen and pour two glasses

of pink lemonade I made this morning. "It's too hot out today," I say. "We're gonna stay inside and play Battleship."

"You're staying home?" Mom's scrunched-up look of worry disappears, replaced by a smile. I couldn't have said anything to make her happier—she'll know where I am every second.

Not that she's been that unbearable lately. I wish I knew what magic words Mrs. Shoshani used when she called Mom on that first day of summer break, because they worked. It's the last week in July, and Dorit and I have been swimming more times than I can even count. And except for the day she showed up at the pool looking for me when I forgot my change for the pay phone and couldn't call her, there haven't been any scenes. Once a week or so, she'll get a killer migraine—one of her many souvenirs from the accident—and I'll feel guilty about having fun while she's miserable. But mostly, I've had a great summer. I love waking up every morning, knowing Dorit's coming over here or I'm going over to her house, and even after we spend a whole day together, we end up gabbing on the phone after dinner.

I set two game cases, one red and one blue, on the table. Dorit paws through the pantry and pulls out a box of powdered sugar doughnuts. "Score!" she says with a giggle. Mom watches us, and I can tell something's spinning around inside her head.

"Yeeessss?" I say.

"I've been thinking about that university trip you mentioned. Two girls traipsing around alone . . . I don't know."

My heart sinks. She's back to ruining every bit of fun for me.

Dorit picks up on my feelings right away and opens her mouth to do some fast talking. But before she can get a word out, the telephone rings. As Mom rushes to answer it, Dorit and I hunker down behind our grids and set up our ships. I'm hoping this'll be a nice long call and Mom will forget all about the university. Heck, we're not even going until the end of August, weeks from now. I shouldn't have even mentioned it to her so soon.

Mom's voice sounds light as she speaks into the phone. "The girls are home today—all set up with Battleship and doughnuts!"

Dad must be calling from work. Good—that'll distract her and put her in a good mood.

"I did," she says after a pause. "And I figured out how to change the tempo too. I'm working through the *Fiddler on the Roof* songbook."

I sort through the pegs in my game box, separating reds from whites, listening to Mom talk.

She chuckles. "Well, I'm not quite ready for Carnegie Hall yet!" She sounds happy. Maybe this keyboard thing really was a good idea.

Dorit looks up at me with steely eyes. "You know I'm gonna crush you, right?"

I let out a *pffft* sound. "You mean like last time, when I blew every one of your ships out of the ocean? Oh, and you begged me for mercy?"

"You wish."

"Have a doughnut," I say. "You're gonna need some extra strength for this round."

She takes a dramatic bite but inhales the coating of the powdered sugar, and it launches her straight into a coughing spell. "Ahh! It's a setup!" she says, hacking away. "You're trying to poison me before we even get started!"

We're both laughing when all of a sudden Mom grows quiet, clutching the phone, her back stiffening.

"What do you mean? You decided without even asking me?" Her words become louder and tinged with anger.

My heart hammers. My parents are going to have a fight.

Mom slips around the doorway of the kitchen and down the basement stairs, only we still hear her because the phone cord barely stretches past the third step.

"How long will you be leaving us for this time? A whole week? Or maybe that's not enough for you." She's spitting the words out at him.

I picture Dad's helpless look. Sometimes he has to go to conferences and meetings, and Mom acts like he's going to die in a fiery crash and never come home.

"Never mind. It doesn't matter how I feel anyway. The lab is always more important than we are."

A lump grows in my throat. Does she really think that's true? I whisk my fingers through the pile of plastic submarines, hoping the rattle will drown out Mom's tirade, but neither of us can pretend we don't hear every word.

"Oh, we'll *definitely* talk about it when you get home," Mom says.

Dorit dumps the game pieces into her case. "Let's go to your room." I grab the box of doughnuts out of spite—Mom hates us eating in our bedrooms—and follow her. I know it's a huge mess, but I don't care.

Once in my bedroom, I push the door closed behind us. "I'm so sorry about that," I say, shoving a pile of clothes against the wall.

"It's fine." She squeezes my arm. "You should've seen my dad lose it the other day when we got separated from him at the mall. None of this is our fault, so don't apologize."

No one has ever said that to me before. *It's not my fault.*

Dorit must know I need time to let her words sink in because she turns away from me and surveys my room. She's been in here tons of times—usually cracking jokes about the mounds of mess being hazardous—but today she takes extra time to look at my troll dolls and candles and dozens of containers of arts-and-crafts supplies. When she picks up one of my prized fossils, it reminds me of the fun our family used to have hiking down to Lake Michigan on the nature preserve path. But it's steep with big drop-offs, so I doubt we'll ever go there again.

"We can play Battleship later," she says once I can finally meet her eyes without feeling like I'm about to cry. "I want to know where you got this cool plant holder." She runs her fingers over the nest of interwoven twine and wooden beads that covers a potted spider plant in the corner.

"I—I made it. Didn't I tell you I'm really into macramé lately?" I don't say that it's because one day at school, the Shimmers were going on about a *Teen Beat* article with instructions for making macramé projects. I came home and found the magazine and taught myself the thread-knotting technique. I've gotten really good at it—like I am at most crafts—even though I never heard the Shimmers ever mention it again.

"You made that? Do you think you can teach me?"

I'm so relieved that we're focused on something besides Mom and Dad's fight that I immediately slide my supply box out from my craft corner and rifle through the containers. "I'm out of jute—that's the brownish rope you use for plant hangers—but I have tons of this floss in all different colors. We could make friendship bracelets." I open up my *Crafty Tweens* book to a page with diagrams. "See?" Soon we're choosing patterns and wrapping string around each other's wrists, measuring our sizes.

I think back to the bracelet I made for Vicky. She thanked me but never wore it, and when I asked her why, she made a face and said it felt itchy on her arm.

I roll up the side of my rug, and Dorit and I tape the knotted threads to the floor so it'll be easier to work with them. After a quick lesson, she's hunched over, weaving strands back and forth and around each other in a pattern of orange and blue and yellow stripes.

Meanwhile, cymbals crash, horns blare, and the walls start to vibrate to some Broadway show tune. But that's nothing compared to the commotion that'll be in our house tonight when Dad comes home.

As if she's reading my mind, Dorit looks up. "Sleepover at my house tonight?"

I can't pack fast enough.

Chapter 7

FACT: EIGHT WEEKS OF SCHOOL ARE ENDLESS math worksheets, vocabulary words, and clocks' hands inching their way around the numbers, but eight weeks of summer are like a dream you can barely even remember when you wake up.

It's a muggy night in August, only a week before school starts up again, and I'm helping Dad wash dishes after the dinner we made together: Mad Hatter Meatballs and Flopsy-Mopsy Carrots. We're a good team with my creativity and his technical skills, which he claims come from being a chemist and knowing how to combine substances without blowing them up. Sometimes I feel like I'm in his lab, the way he slices perfect cubes of vegetables and heats liquids to an exact simmer.

When the doorbell rings its friendly little *ping*, Mom flinches.

"It's all right, Mommy," I say. "That's just Dorit. She's coming over to hear my new Carpenters album."

Jon yells, "I'll answer it!" from the living room, and I think I hear him tear himself away from our new color TV. Most of the time he can't keep his paws off of it. It's huge, like a piece of furniture, with a wooden frame around it and knobs you can turn to make the colors brighter or pinker or bluer.

"Drink your water," Dad tells Mom as he arranges wet dishes on the drainer. "After all that vomiting today, you better not get dehydrated." She nods and winces, bringing her hand up to her flattened hair. Ice cubes clink as she sips from a tall glass.

"Still have the headache?" I ask, but I already know the answer. I squeeze onto the chair with her, my head resting on her shoulder. Times like this make me want to snuggle close and promise I'll be more patient when she worries.

The doorbell *ping*s again.

"Hold on! I'm tuning our fabulous new solid-state color TV," yells Jon.

I swear, he's obsessed. "I'll get it," I say, sliding away from Mom. I swing our front door open and greet Dorit. "Sorry for making you wait. Jon can't pry himself off our new TV."

"I need to get this picture to work in time for President Nixon's speech," Jon announces, on his knees.

"Like I even care? Do you realize that while Dorit

and I perfected our dives and learned to play tennis, all you did for the past eight weeks was watch Watergate hearings?"

"Yeah—too bad you wasted your summer. You may be able to lob a little ball over a net, but I'll bet you don't know who Alexander Butterfield is." He wiggles a knob, finally bringing the picture into focus.

"Oh, sure. Everyone knows good old Alexander Butterfield. I love his new song—I think it hit number one this week!" I can't contain my snickering. "Dad," I call into the kitchen, "do you know who Alexander Butterfield is?"

Dad pokes his head into the living room. "Why? Is *he* at our door?" He laughs, proud of his joke.

"Argh! Come on, Mel, wake up," says Jon. "He's the guy who let the big secret out: President Nixon's been secretly taping everyone in the White House! He has recordings of all his private conversations. If the Senate can manage to listen to them, they could find out if he's been lying."

"So why don't they ask for his tapes? I don't get why this is such a big deal."

Jon sighs like I'm asking why there isn't world peace, so Dad pipes in.

"President Nixon refuses to turn them over." He wipes his hands on the dish towel tucked around his waist. "There must be something on those tapes that will get him in trouble, so he's making excuses about why no one can listen to them."

Jon shakes his head, furrows his eyebrows, and does his best presidential impression like the comedians on TV. "VERY SENSITIVE INFORMATION ON THOSE TAPES, VITAL TO OUR NATIONAL SECURITY!" He turns a big knob, and the words *SPECIAL NEWS REPORT* blaze across the screen. "Finally!"

"Is this gonna be on all three channels?" I ask. He turns from NBC to ABC, and then to CBS, and it's everywhere. I groan. "Shoot! I'm so sick of Watergate!"

"Never mind," Dorit whispers. "I have news about tomorrow! My abba finally agreed that we can go around the art museum without him! Come downstairs so we can talk more."

I let out a squeal. I've only pictured her father tailing us all day. It'll be so much cooler to go to the university alone. Although Mom would have a cow if she knew.

As Dorit pulls me out of the living room, she hands me something. "Look what I got at Record City." It's the hot pink card with *WLAK's Super Top 40 Hits* printed at the top. It comes out every week, and we've been following it all summer. "I didn't know if you saw the new one yet."

"Wow," I say. "'Yesterday Once More' is number four. Go Carpenters!"

"And 'Monster Mash' is *still* in the top ten." Dorit sings the opening line in her best Dracula accent. We both crack up.

When we reach the kitchen, Mom's holding a washcloth to her forehead. Dorit murmurs, "Is . . . is it okay that I'm here?"

I love that I don't have to make up excuses or keep her from seeing when Mom's not doing so well. Maybe someday I'll feel that way with everybody. Maybe someday Mom won't be like this.

"Are you kidding?" I grab her arm. "You're saving me from another speech by President Nixon. Let's go to the basement! The new Carpenters album is awesome—we can try out some harmonies."

"Keep it down or every dog in the neighborhood's going to be howling." Jon laughs at his own joke as he adjusts the TV volume.

As the president's "Good evening" fills our living room, our doorbell rings again, followed by a string of knocks that turns into pounds. Mom groans as if each thump hits her head. "What in the world is going on?" she says. The doorbell's *ping*s come fast now, one after another. I race from the kitchen to answer it.

"Let me in!" calls someone on the other side of the door.

I'd know that raspy voice anywhere.

Perched on the front step, wearing mini shorts and a sparkly *Hollywood* T-shirt, stands Vicky. She looks older. She looks amazing.

"You're back!" I throw my arms around her.

She squeezes me. "I just got home." But one step into our house, she stiffens and steps away from me. "Oh! I didn't realize you had company."

"Just Dorit," I say, and right away I feel awful. "I mean, you're not interrupting us."

Dorit gives a half-hearted wave. "Yeah. We were about to listen to the new Carpenters album."

Shoot. I've hurt her feelings.

Vicky laughs. "Oh, God—you like them? In California we listened to—"

"Hey, pipe down. We're trying to hear the TV." Jon turns around, but instead of shooting a "shut up" look at Vicky, he does a double take.

She flips her hair and smiles. "Wow, Jon—when did you become such a grown-up?"

"It's . . . it's an important speech." His cheeks flame as he whips his head back toward the screen, and Vicky cracks up.

President Nixon's voice fills our house. ". . . and I state again, to every one of you listening tonight, these facts: I had no prior knowledge of the Watergate break-in."

"Liar!" Jon growls. "You oughtta be impeached! Turn over the tapes!"

"Jon, shh! Show some respect; it's the president," Mom scolds.

President Nixon reads his boring speech from a sheet of paper while we stand here watching. Dorit finally taps me and eyes the basement door.

"Do you want to come down with us?" I ask Vicky, even though I'm not sure that's a good idea. This is already so awkward—the three of us together for the first time since summer began. No matter who I talk to, it's going to feel like I'm ignoring someone.

"No, thanks. I'd rather unpack my dirty clothes than listen to a whole album by the Carpenters. Besides, I told my parents I'd only stop by for a minute."

Dorit runs fingers through her ponytail. "Gee," she says, "tell us how you *really* feel."

Vicky ignores her remark. "Walk me to the end of the block. I have something to tell you." Vicky links her arm through mine and whispers, but it's loud enough for Dorit to hear.

Dorit looks at us as if we're speeding along in a car and she knows I'm about to shove her out the door.

I want to tell Vicky, "*No*, I can't drop everything for you," but I've noticed the way her eyes sparkle, and I'm curious. Maybe something big happened in California.

"I'll only be gone for a second," I tell Dorit. "Why don't you go downstairs and set up the record?" Jon and Mom watch as she opens the basement door. Mom gives me a disapproving look that Vicky catches. My armpits grow all itchy.

"We're only walking to the end of the block," Vicky tells Mom. "And it's not even dark yet." For once, though, that's not what Mom's unhappy about.

Outside, Vicky struts like she won a prize—which, I guess, is me. Or maybe it's knowing she can still get me to do whatever she wants. "Mel, you look super terrific! Your hair grew, like, a foot, and you have a tan!"

"Yeah, I guess." I finger through my bangs, lighter from all those days at the pool. I glance back toward my house. I should've stayed.

We pass the house across the street, the *FOR SALE* sign still stuck in the front lawn.

"So how was California?" I ask. "I mean, the quick version."

She sticks out her bronzed leg. "Awesome. We spent every day at the beach. Look at my tan. And I took a million pictures, but I'll show you later, when you're not *busy*."

Should I tell her about my awesome summer? I'd never be able to convince her that hanging out with Dorit every day was fun.

I stop at the corner. "I really should go back. What did you want to tell me?"

Vicky plants her hands on my shoulders. "You're coming with me to Wilson Park."

"The one on Lake Michigan, with the private beach?"

"Bingo! Jan called and invited me while I was in California. The Shimmers'll all be there playing volleyball, and Jan's parents are throwing a cookout."

My heart flutters. I wish it wouldn't, but it does.

I think about how they all laughed at me by the high dive. And how last week when Dorit and I walked into The Scoop, Shari whispered something to Marla and they looked at us and giggled. Plus I'm horrible at volleyball. Every time I try to serve, I hit the ball into the net.

"No one invited me. I can't just show up."

Vicky squeezes my shoulders tightly, the way she only does when she's serious. "*I'm* inviting you. Mel, when I was in California, I decided something big: This is our year. You're dying to be a Shimmer. And if you don't become one by eighth grade, forget about high school. It'll be too late."

It's embarrassing to admit, but everything inside me tingles. I never imagined Vicky thinking I could be a Shimmer. I only pictured us growing apart.

But now there's Dorit. The few times I even mentioned the Shimmers this summer, she always turned it into a joke. She thought I agreed, that I was over them.

But she's wrong. *I want it.* And Vicky's dangling it in front of me like a frosted doughnut.

The streetlights flicker. "I really have to go home," I say, walking backward. "When's this happening, anyway?"

"Tomorrow afternoon. A last blast before school starts."

I stumble over a rock. I can't cancel my plans with Dorit.

"What's the matter? Something more important on your social calendar?"

"I . . . I'll call you in the morning," I say. It's all I can come up with. I don't know what I'm supposed to do.

Inside, Mom's sitting straighter. She glances up from the Sears catalog, open to the page of maxi dresses I bookmarked. Rosh Hashanah's only a few weeks away. "I don't know what's going on with Vicky," Mom says. "She used to be so sweet."

"Nah, she's always been a pain in the neck," Jon

says. "What'd she say to you out there anyway? You've got a funny look on your face."

"Mind your own business, Mr. Mature."

Down in the basement, Dorit's on the rug, studying the jacket of *Now and Then*. "Thanks for ditching me." There's nothing jokey about her voice.

"I only walked her to the end of the block," I say, but my neck feels hot and prickly.

"More like *she* walked *you*. Do you even know how to stand up to her? Once she showed up, you acted like I wasn't even there."

Dorit can't possibly understand how I feel right now. It's not like our summer together has been fake or unimportant—it's been the most awesome summer of my life. For sure, she's my best friend. But I don't think I can give up wanting to be a Shimmer for her. As far as I know, she's supposed to be happy for me if it ever comes true.

"I'm really sorry," I finally say. "She just got home and came straight over here, so how could I *not* spend a little time with her?" My heart does a dance of joy when I imagine going to Wilson Park, playing volleyball with Shari and Marla, making jokes about Miss Roole while I'm spiking the ball over the net. I picture them saving a seat for me at a picnic table where we gobble down hamburgers and lemonade.

"Well, don't forget about tomorrow," Dorit says. "I had the fight of the century with my abba last night so we could spend the day without him babysitting us. And whatever you do, don't mention that detail to your mom."

Instead of soaring like it did a few minutes ago, now my heart sinks. "Don't worry," I say, "I'll be there." At the boring art museum.

The black disc of the record drops to the turntable and spins around. The first song on the Carpenters album is called "Sing." There's a part where little kids' voices sing a verse together. It reminds me of summers when everyone in our grade was still friends, and we all played together.

Chapter 8

THE NEXT MORNING I DON'T EVEN NEED AN alarm to wake me. Mom's downstairs at her keyboard, struggling to play some classical piece that comes out sounding like it's from *Creature Features*, that scary late-night TV show.

I slink into the kitchen and eye the phone. I could call Dorit and cancel. I could say I don't feel well or that Mom changed her mind about letting me go.

It's hard to ignore the prickly feeling in my stomach that reminds me how much I'm aching to go to the Shimmers' barbecue, how completely different I could feel there. Nothing heavy or serious. Only swimming, sun, and volleyball. But a promise is a promise, and besides, this outing is really important to Dorit. Before I can do something mean, I call Vicky, and she answers on the first ring.

"Good morning!"

"You're up early," I say. "Aren't you still on California time?"

"My brothers reminded me how they walked Toby all summer, so today I got stuck with the honors. So what time do you want to leave? We can ride our bikes, or my mom can drop us off on her way to the store."

I wind the coiled phone cord around my finger and brace myself. "Here's the thing," I say. "It turns out I can't go. Dorit and I are spending the day at the university art museum. We planned it weeks ago."

Vicky snorts. "You're kidding me, right? You're willing to blow an actual chance to become a Shimmer because of some boring plans you made with Dorit? Don't complain to me next time they call you Miss Model Student."

My heart pounds. I might be making the biggest mistake ever.

Mr. Shoshani pulls the newly repaired station wagon up to University Avenue. I can't get Vicky's voice out of my head.

"You can let us out by the front steps," Dorit says. "I know my way around from here."

"I'll come three o'clock, bidyuk, to this exact spot," her father says, looking us both in the eyes. "If there's trouble, go straight to my office." After we climb out,

I see him watching us from the curb for a long time before he pulls away.

Dorit leads me up the stairs to a modern-looking building, all white, with a twisted sculpture in front. A lady wearing a badge hands us each a map and a sheet of paper that lists the special exhibits.

I feel trapped—trapped in this building, trapped in my life. I'm a goody-goody teacher's pet with a weird family, and I'm scared that's all I'll ever be.

"C'mon," says Dorit, waving me into the main gallery. It's so quiet. All I hear is the echo of footsteps and muffled voices. The walls are filled with gigantic canvases, all painted dark, solid colors: black, gray, maroon. Dorit takes everything in, her face full of awe, like Jon's when we were little and visited the Grand Canyon. After I look them over, I stand around, waiting and watching her. She takes forever. "See what I mean?" she whispers eventually. "Isn't it the coolest feeling, being here?"

Thrilling. "I don't get it," I admit. "They mostly look like my old preschool art projects."

Dorit's neck grows pink and splotchy. I know I sound bratty. "They're contemporary," she says. "Don't you feel anything when you look at them?"

I shrug. I hate that I'm acting like this, but I can't shake my grumpy mood.

"What about this one?" she asks, pointing to a black

canvas with a big red blob, the color of blood, in the center. "Doesn't it make you consider the hopelessness of the human condition?" She raises her hand to her forehead. "So . . . terrible!" Breaking into a round of giggles, she looks at me expectantly, like I'll laugh too.

Instead, I scrunch up my face. "That *artist* is terrible. Why do you even like these?"

"Maybe you need to give it a chance," she says. I can tell she's annoyed. "Come on, I'll show you the ones I like best—they're upstairs."

I trudge up the marble steps behind her, one after another, until we reach a bright gallery. We stop at every painting, stepping closer to examine the brushstrokes and to read signs with the artists' names. Some are of flowers, and some are of sunsets. The one of a lady wearing a big hat has a fancy gold frame.

They *are* beautiful, but I won't admit that I'm impressed. "These look like the posters in your bedroom." My voice is flat.

"You're right. These artists are from the same period." Dorit's answer is short and icy. She heads into the hallway and into another exhibit, leaving me behind.

We tour the museum separately. I walk past heavy, dark paintings of people who look like kings and queens. Next I find myself surrounded by muddy green and brown scenes of rivers and fields. I spot Dorit every few minutes, but neither makes a move toward the other. It's not the way either of us pictured the day going.

When we finally meet up in the glass art collection, she's frowning. "You're having a rotten time, aren't you?"

She's so right. It's boring and stuffy, and all I'm thinking about is how I could be spending my day if I weren't here. I know she's disappointed, and I wanted to be a good sport and keep my promise, but frustration bubbles up around me like sewer water in a storm.

"If you really don't like this, we could go someplace more fun on campus. There's a lot to see."

"What about your dad?"

"He'll be in his office. He'll never know."

I straighten up and glance toward the exit sign where a map of the campus is posted. An idea is growing inside me. "Okay . . . then how about *I* pick our next stop? Close your eyes and I'll surprise you." I can't wait to get out of this museum.

As soon as we're down the stairs, I pull her along, her eyes shut, across the grassy center of campus where an old columned building sits on each corner. "Where are we going?" she asks. "I didn't think you even knew your way around here."

"There's a place I remember from a field trip. You'll love it. Wait till you see." I drag her through the doors of the biggest one, Jefferson Hall.

"This place smells really familiar," she says. "Musty and gross. You sure you didn't take me back to my brothers' room?"

I can't stop laughing. "Open your eyes."

"Oh, yuck! This is disgusting!"

The case is full of dead cockroaches, part of the Holtzman Collection in the natural history department. Rows of shiny brown bugs with gross legs and antennas glint at us.

I'm cracking up. She's not.

"Why do you think it's funny?" The next wall holds display cases full of squirrels and wolves and deer standing in Styrofoam snow.

"I just like it better than your favorite paintings, I guess." A part of me wants to push her away and see what she'll do. Maybe she'll get so mad that we'll leave, and then I can go to Wilson Park.

Her cheeks turn pink. She walks over to the Birds of the Midwest display full of different shapes of nests and different-colored eggs. "What's your problem today? This isn't funny. You're being really rude. If you didn't want to come, why didn't you say so?"

Suddenly I feel awful. Today was supposed to be special. We've talked about it since June, and I'm ruining it.

"Why are you acting so weird? Did I do something to make you mad?"

I stay quiet for a long time. I can't tell her the truth—she'd never understand. It would make her angrier. "I'm sorry," I finally say. "I . . . I guess I'm in a bad mood. My mom calls it Attack of the Hormones." It's partially true. Last night I ate a whole row of Oreos, and a sappy Hallmark commercial made me cry.

Dorit nods like she finally understands, but I feel rotten because she really doesn't.

"Let's start over," I say. "Maybe we can find something we *both* like."

Dorit gazes out the window at the campus below while I wait, hoping I haven't completely spoiled the day. When she turns back toward me, her face brightens. "I have an idea," she says.

A few blocks down, past the business building and the English department, we reach a brick structure, almost deserted except for a few stray students wandering around.

"This is, like, the main place where you hang out if you go to school here," Dorit says. "Isn't it cool? There's a bowling alley with eight lanes." She leads me down the steps. "Plus a mini movie theater, a cafeteria, and even a place to sit and watch TV." I crane my head to take it all in. How could I have lived in Ashford my whole life and never known about this?

"Here's the best thing," Dorit says, pointing to the

sign for the university ice-cream parlor. "This place is even better than The Scoop."

We slide into a booth, and the waitress hands us laminated menus. "These are as big as posters! How're we supposed to decide?" My grumpiness is lifting. If I can't be at Wilson Park, at least there's ice cream.

"Let's have something enormous," says Dorit. "No one here knows us, so we don't have to worry about anyone judging us."

No one here knows us. When she says that, suddenly I'm in my bikini, with Shari and Marla and the rest of the Shimmers, playing volleyball and eating burgers. Vicky's watching to make sure I don't do anything uncool. Honestly, that part sounds awful—having to worry about how I look and sound every second. It may even be too late for me to become a Shimmer; I'm already Miss Model Student with the mom who worries about everything, and maybe that's how I'm supposed to stay. Maybe that's even okay.

"Let's split the largest sundae on the menu!" says Dorit. "I've been dying to try it with someone. It's sixteen scoops!" She looks so excited, so full of giggles, that it makes me laugh.

"Let's go for it!"

When the waitress brings it, Dorit says, "Wow, too bad I don't have a camera."

"I've never seen so much ice cream!" I plunge in: eating, cracking up, licking my lips. "Oh, man, my sides hurt. It's so much to eat."

"Mmm! Try the caramel brownie and butter brickle together," Dorit says.

"Here—take this little pitcher. You have to pour hot fudge on top."

"And some maraschino cherries."

"Try it with butterscotch."

By the time we've each eaten the last spoonful we can manage, our hands and faces are a sticky mess.

Our waitress brings us warm towelettes to wipe our hands. "I think you need showers here," I joke.

After we pay our bill at the front counter, we pool our change and leave a tip on our table. The hostess leads us to the door, a key ring dangling from her wrist. "We close at three until the students return. You just made it under the wire!"

"It's three already?" Dorit grabs me. "We're supposed to meet my abba in front of the art museum right now!"

By the time we reach the museum, we're drenched in sweat, but we're also cracking up.

"Remember," she whispers as we climb into the station wagon, "we were here the whole time."

But I wasn't.

And I'm realizing you can't be in two places at once.

Chapter 9

IN THE AUDITORIUM ON THE FIRST DAY BACK TO
school, Dorit pops out of her seat and waves. "Melanie, over here!" Her eyes and nose are puffy and pink. "Hay fever—it's horrible," she explains, pulling a tissue out of her pocket.

Miss Roole wheels a blackboard across the empty stage. *Welcome to the 1973–74 School Year!* is written in bold chalky letters.

Dorit flashes her half sheet of paper. "So cool—computer-printed schedules. I heard they're computerizing everything soon: the library, attendance . . ." She pokes me. "Mel, are you listening?"

But I'm not. I'm staring at the back row where the Shimmers are gathered. I saw them around Ashford over the summer, but right now, standing all together, they look so *mature*: the girls in their hip-hugger bell-bottoms, the boys in faded Levi's.

I feel like a wave has swallowed me and spit me back to shore. All of a sudden, my summer with Dorit feels completely babyish. We ran through her sprinkler in play shorts and rode together on my bike to the pool, while they won swim meets and threw parties.

When the bell rings, Miss Roole jumps right in. "Seats, people. And schedules out." Her eyes zero in on the Shimmers. "Quiet in the back! Let me know when you're ready. I can wait here all day." She bends to pick up a stray paper, and her hair stays perfectly still, as if she'd brushed it with Mod Podge.

"We'd better be together for something." Dorit scans my paper as Miss Roole flips the blackboard and scrawl-taps with her chalk, trying to explain what it all means.

There are codes for different days of the week and codes for every teacher. Most of it looks like a kid got ahold of chalk and scribbled random numbers and letters on the board. Why can't they just print out the class names?

I figure out that *ENG8-1* means eighth-grade English, Section 1. *GRFD-8* means Girls' Foods for eighth grade, and *SOC8-2* is Section 2 of Social Studies. Dorit's schedule has a matching *SOC8-2* printed in bold letters. "We're in Mr. Pitkewicz's class together," I say. "I've heard horror stories about how hard he is."

"The Pits doesn't scare me," says Dorit. I believe her.

Miss Roole launches into her tired beginning-of-the-year speech. At the part about knuckling down and making this our best year ever, Vicky strolls in, dropping into the empty seat in front of us. "I missed the bus. Don't tell me we're getting this pointless pep talk again." She unzips her book bag and pulls out her schedule. "You don't mind if I sit over here, do you?" She shoots Dorit a knowing look. "I hope the university was more fun than going to the Shimmers' cookout."

Dorit's eyes snap toward me. "Now I know why you were acting so weird."

Of course, Vicky couldn't resist a chance to create drama.

"Don't listen to her," I whisper. "We had fun." I want to convince her, like I want to convince myself. Wilson Park with the Shimmers . . . I may never have the chance again.

Dorit sends Vicky the stink eye. "I'm not giving her the satisfaction of getting mad about it," she mutters. "That's what she wants."

Someone squeals, and the whole auditorium turns to see. It's Marla and Aaron Andrews, locked in an arm-wrestling match. Vicky gapes at them. "I can't believe it."

"I know," I say. "They look like they're in high school."

She shakes her head. "No, you tadpole—I always thought he liked *me*."

Like the scramble of letters and numbers on my schedule, eighth grade already feels complicated.

★ ★ ★

I hate how school starts with a bang: teachers pile on the homework right away, coming down hard and heavy with their rules (which totally scare a law-abider like me), but a few days later, we have a long weekend because it's Labor Day.

The weather is always super hot, and there are no classes, but it feels nothing like summer vacation. For one thing, the pool's closed for the season. We also have vocab quizzes to study for and algebra worksheets to finish, and we know we're not sleeping in the next morning. It's like being stuck between two big things.

Even more, though, I hate how it feels like nothing's changed since last year. As close as Dorit and I became this summer, the second I saw the Shimmers in the auditorium, I knew I still wanted to be one. Dorit sensed it right away too, and that's why I feel horrible. What kind of best friend am I, spending the perfect summer with her and then acting like it wasn't enough as soon as I see the cool kids again?

As Dorit and I stand in the Kwik-Mart on Labor Day afternoon, a pang of regret hits me. Dorit listens every time I freak out about Mom. She knows exactly when I need to get out of my house and clear my mind. She's always ready to talk about deep topics, like why awful things happen to good people. She's hilarious, whether we're doing cannonballs at the pool or telling spooky stories at sleepovers. I could spend an entire day with her, and as soon as she'd leave I'd wish she were still here. Vicky and I may have been best friends since we were little, but Vicky will never understand my family the way Dorit does.

I finish my pretzel and toss a napkin into the garbage can. Dorit shoves her slushie at me. "Have a drink. Maybe it'll pull you out of your grouchy mood."

"I'm not grouchy," I answer, maybe too fast.

"Well, there's someplace cool I've been wanting to show you." Dorit shakes out the last drops from her cup. "And I'll need this once we get there."

"Huh?"

"You'll see," she says. "Let's make it into an adventure. After we cross the street, close your eyes and I'll take you there. And don't worry—I'm not taking you to a museum to see a bunch of dead bugs."

I cringe when she says that. I don't want to act obnoxious like I did on the day we visited the university.

At the sidewalk, I clutch her arm while she leads me forward. "I have to give you credit," I say, trying to adjust my attitude. "I can't picture any place in Ashford where I've never been before."

"Well, it's not *exactly* Ashford," she says, "but I'm not giving away any more clues."

We walk and walk. Sweat beads around my forehead. "How far have we gone?"

"Only a few blocks, Miss Antsy. I'll let you know when we're close."

The minutes pass. She's still pulling me.

"I'm getting thirsty," I say.

"You drank half of my slushie. I think you'll survive."

It feels like we've walked ten miles. "Do you even know where we're going?"

Dorit clears her throat. "I think we only have a bit more to go."

"You *think*?"

She giggles. "It's kind of out of the way, and I usually come with my brothers, so I might not remember exactly how to get there."

"You're kidding me—right?"

"Relax! I think it's looking familiar."

I listen hard to the sounds around me, but I only hear the usual: the singsong voices of kids playing, lawnmowers rumbling, and cars passing by. Nothing that tells me where we're headed.

Finally, Dorit's footsteps wind down. Grass tickles my ankles, and something bumpy, like gravel, pokes at the soles of my shoes. Sunshine warms my face.

"Here we are," says Dorit. "I knew I could find it again."

"Can I look now?"

"Go for it," she says.

It takes my eyes a second to adjust to the brilliance of the light after being closed tight, but once the dazzling golds and silvers come into view, it's obvious where Dorit has brought me.

"I don't get it," I say. "Is this a joke?"

"What do you mean? Isn't it beautiful? And check out the rocks. That's why I brought the cup. I'm going to dig up some of those shiny ones for my brothers."

In the distance, a gazebo is packed with families having a cookout. I recognize Shari in her floppy hat. And Marla. And Jan. And Aaron Andrews and Jerry Finkel. And a bunch of parents and a gaggle of little kids—probably their siblings—playing tag. A picnic table is piled with food, and the smell of barbecue drifts into the air.

"Dorit, this is Shimmer Pond. Don't you know?"

She shrugs, unimpressed. "My first time here,

I wondered if that's what it might be. But there's no sign telling me to curtsey and show proper respect for the royalty. It just looks like a really pretty lake."

I yank her arm. "We can't stay."

"Why not?"

I'll die if the Shimmers think I'm stalking their party. All I need is for Jerry to tease me in front of everyone. "They . . . they're having a picnic. It looks private."

"This park is public. You're being silly." She marches down to the pond and surveys the shore, plucking rocks and dropping them into her cup. "C'mon down." She looks like a toddler playing in the mud. I want to disappear.

I sink into the grass. I don't even want to yell "I'm staying here!" because it might attract the Shimmers' attention. Off in the distance, across the street, their tall brick houses line the park. I'm not sure which one belongs to each of them, but I know none are like mine. No one's parents are fighting. Their moms aren't wandering around at night, checking if they're safe in bed.

As Dorit picks up her cup and scans the shore, I try to hold her and the Shimmers in my view at the same time. I wish she'd give them a chance. I wish she'd understand why I want to be one of them and promise we'd stay friends if that happened.

Seconds later, she jogs back up to where I'm sitting. "Check out these beauties." She dumps her cup at my feet. "I found some granite and even some red jasper."

"Can we leave now?"

Ignoring the distress in my voice, she eases down next to me. She even unties her shoes and loosens them like we're staying for a while. When she leans back onto her elbows, the sun catches the red highlights in her hair. "You know, they're just a group of families having a picnic."

A woman Mom's age pulls Marla over to an older couple who hug her. Little kids scramble onto Shari's lap. Some guy piles a stack of dirty plates into Jerry's arms and directs him to the garbage can. She's right. If I didn't know them, they'd look ordinary.

They're just kids like me. I say it in my head.

I wish I could believe it.

Chapter 10

MY HOMEROOM TEACHER, MS. LOOMIS, STRIDES into the classroom wearing a T-shirt with the words *Go, Billie, Go!* on it. "Let's hear it for Billie Jean, ladies! If she can do it, so can you!"

Several boys groan.

She's talking about how Billie Jean King crushed Bobby Riggs in tennis last night. On the news they called it "The Battle of the Sexes," and said thirty thousand people packed into the Astrodome to watch, like it was the World Series or Super Bowl. I watched it on TV, along with every other kid at school.

Lots of people say women athletes shouldn't get paid as much as men because they're not as important. Billie Jean has to be so sure of herself. She stands strong no matter how many people oppose her. I wish I could be like that.

In social studies, Mr. Pitkewicz is business as usual, adjusting his wire glasses and moving to the center of the room. "Seats, people!" He claps his hands together. "We're starting World War I today!"

Jerry jumps out of his seat, yelling, "Hit the trenches!" Everyone around me cracks up, and by everyone, I mean the Shimmers.

I want to catch Shari's eye, to laugh with her and whisper something funny about The Pits, but even if I picture Billie Jean King throwing her racket up in victory, I can't do it. It's like I'm on a tennis court for the first time and balls are whizzing past me in all directions.

"Let's rethink that, Mr. Finkel," says Mr. Pitkewicz, pulling the classroom door closed and lowering the blinds.

The class grows quiet. It didn't take us long to discover that The Pits is the hardest teacher in school even though he looks like he's in college, with his long hair and round "granny glasses."

He plays a fuzzy black-and-white movie that shows tanks barreling through cities. Behind me, Shari and Marla compare nails and debate polish colors. When it's over, The Pits clicks a switch, and the projector hums as the reels reverse directions and rewind the film. The room is still.

"Anyone awake?" He passes out thick packets of paper. "This'll perk you up."

I flip through the pages: over a hundred terms to explain or define, plus a list of essay questions about the long- and short-range causes of the war. Jerry lets out a massive groan and murmurs "The Pits is a maniac" under his breath.

"Any questions, Mr. Finkel?"

"Yeah," he says. "How many years do we get to finish this?" Shimmers laugh all around me.

"You'll have ample time," says Mr. Pitkewicz, "and the Ashford Library has all the reference materials you'll need. Get to know it."

When the bell rings, Dorit zips over. "You want to work together at the library?" She looks like she can't wait to get started. "We can go early and grab the best study room, and I heard about this bakery across the street with the most amazing doughnuts—"

"It's Gleason's," Vicky says, stopping next to us. "Been there a thousand times. But you're kidding, right? You don't have anything better to do than spend your free time at the library?" She looks at Jan, and they both roll their eyes.

My neck grows hot as they brush past us. I can't help feeling embarrassed that Dorit's so excited to start our project. And ever since the Wilson Park incident, things are still tense with Vicky. Instead of helping me with the Shimmers, sometimes it seems like she's trying to make me look bad in front of them.

"Vicky really can't stand me, can she?" says Dorit. She states it like it's just a fact, not like it bothers her. She even smiles. "She's so jealous that we're friends."

"No way," I say instinctively. "She's never been jealous of anything about me." But I know that's not true.

"I can see stuff that you can't," says Dorit.

"Can you see how freaked out I am about this project?"

"Stop worrying," she says. "We can do anything, remember? Like Billie Jean King."

"Yeah, I'd like to see her do one of The Pits's assignments."

Chapter 11

ON SATURDAY TWO WEEKS LATER, I'M LYING IN bed, trying not to think about breakfast—or food in general—or how thirsty I am. It's Yom Kippur, the Day of Atonement, when we spend all day in synagogue fasting and praying for forgiveness of all our sins over the past year. We're not a super-religious family: we never talk about God, and we don't go to temple every week— mostly when we're invited to a bar or bat mitzvah. But I can't remember us ever *not* going for Yom Kippur.

I mean, we're very Jewish, as in bagels and lox, *Fiddler on the Roof*, Hanukkah presents, and all that. Whenever famous Jewish people, like Barbra Streisand or Bob Dylan, are in the news or in a movie, Mom always points them out to me. Jon even had a bar mitzvah with a band and a luncheon, and all our out-of-town relatives came. I started Hebrew school after our car accident. The temple's minibus picked me up after school because Mom wouldn't drive, and since our neighbors all belonged to a different temple, I had to ride with kids I didn't know. I begged to quit right around the time Mom needed another surgery, and my parents finally caved and decided it was one less thing to deal with.

I wish I had stayed to learn all the prayers and to read Hebrew like Jon does—and to ask the rabbi and teachers questions like "How could a loving God let my mom get hurt so badly?" Because we sure don't talk about it at home. We don't talk about a lot of things that are deep and emotional. That's the way my parents are.

Mom may worry and tell me to be careful and not let me go places alone, but she never says it's because she loves me so much and is terrified of losing me. Not showing those feelings doesn't mean they aren't there, though. I still feel sad lots of mornings when I see Mom lying in bed, even if neither of us talks about it.

That's why I'm surprised when I hear her suck in her breath and wail, "Oh no! I can't believe it!"

My blankets tumble to the floor, and in an instant, I'm through her doorway. "What's the matter?" She's sitting up against her headboard, holding the telephone receiver to her ear. I can't tell what's wrong. Maybe her headaches are getting worse.

I turn toward Dad, who's also in the room. "What's happening? Is Mom okay?"

He rubs his forehead. "Grandma Esther called from New York. The radio just reported that Egypt and Syria attacked Israel today. They're at war."

Nothing's wrong with Mom. Relief pounds in my chest.

Until I think about Dorit. I wonder if her family knows. I think her grandparents still live there.

After Mom hangs up, I slip into her bed and hug her long and hard.

"Did Dad tell you?" Her words are muffled against my neck.

"Yeah," I say, but Dad's knotting his tie, and Mom looks okay—she doesn't need a doctor. Nothing's *really* wrong. Mom slides out of bed and twists the knob on the television, passing cartoons and commercials until *SPECIAL NEWS REPORT* flashes across the screen. A map shows Israel, Egypt, and Syria, with arrows and dotted lines drawn crisscrossing the countries.

It's far from here, like Vietnam. Up until last year, every night on the news, Walter Cronkite announced the number of American soldiers killed that day in places like Saigon and Hanoi, which I can picture about as easily as I can picture Jupiter. Still, I wore a silver wristband stamped with the name of a prisoner of war and his date of capture. Mine was Ronald Bolt, 5-9-72. I once wrote his family a letter. I think about his wife sometimes; she's the one who wrote back.

"Hey, turn the sound up," says Jon, his curly hair still flattened on one side of his head. He sniffs out news like Vicky's dog, Toby, can track down a package of hot dogs.

"*Combined Egyptian and Syrian forces launch a surprise attack on Israel on Yom Kippur, the holiest day in Judaism. Once again, the Middle East is at war.*"

A crowd jams into the temple lobby. I wish I could talk to Dorit, but her family doesn't go here.

"Shanah tovah, Melanie," someone says. The moms look so different dressed in stiff blazers and pointy heels instead of their everyday clothes. Perfume scents mingle in the air.

The girls fidget in their dresses and nylons, and the boys are stuffed into shirts and ties, whacking one another with their satin yarmulkes. Vicky's family comes late every year—like that's a surprise—and the only Shimmer I see is Jan Rosen. I think the others go to the synagogue in Highland Hills. Jan's standing next to two boys with the same color hair as hers, probably her brothers. I fluff out my maxi dress that Mom bought me from the Sears catalog, and I look straight at her. Nothing. Not even a flicker in her eyes to show she recognizes me.

Voices echo off lobby walls like the room is humming, but once I'm inside the carpeted sanctuary, there are only creaks and dull thumps while people settle into their movie-theater-type seats.

The rabbi says, "By now, most of you have heard the terrible news that Israel is at war." A murmur runs through the crowd. Some people must be just finding out. "We must have faith that God will protect the Jews, shielding His people beneath the wings of his love and spreading it over a canopy of peace."

After the rabbi's sermon, Mr. Buckman from the hardware store asks everyone to donate money to a relief fund being set up for war victims. More whispers travel through the crowd.

"How does that look?" I ask Dad later, handing him a plate with a perfectly folded omelet. "Just the thing to break the fast, huh?"

He raises a forkful of egg and gooey cheese and takes a bite. "Delicious."

"Sit down," says Mom. "Who do you have to call while we're eating?"

"Dorit. We're working on social studies at the library tomorrow. And . . . I'll bet her family's worried about what's going on in Israel." An uneasy feeling swirls around in my middle. I hope everything's all right.

I sit on the basement stairs, a plate in my lap, the phone cord stretched to its limit. One busy signal sounds after another until I finally give up for the night.

In the morning, I still can't reach her. Dad throws on his jacket, ready to drop me off for a boring day alone at the library. I tell Mom I'm meeting Vicky, which is a joke—no way would she give up a Sunday for schoolwork.

"You ready, Mel?" Dad's jingling his keys. Sundays are big home repair and errand days, and he's ready to go.

"Can I try her one last time?" I ask, dialing Dorit's number. "I promise I'll be quick." I jiggle the metal tab on my windbreaker while her phone actually rings this time.

Dorit answers right away, as if she'd been sitting next to the phone, waiting for a call.

"Finally!" I say. "Your line's been busy for, like, *forever*! Is everything okay?"

"Who is it?" her brother yells in the background.

"It's Melanie," whispers Dorit, adding something in Hebrew that I don't understand.

"Hey, are you there? You've been impossible to reach."

"I can only talk for a second. We're waiting to hear from my grandparents."

I press the phone against my ear. "That's what I was afraid of." Dad gives me a let's-get-going look.

"Yeah," she says. The hiss of silence is thick. "We called people all day yesterday to check if they're okay, but they don't have a phone. We need to keep our line free in case they try to reach us."

"Should I . . . Do you want me to come over and wait—"

"No! I mean, it's okay. *I'm* okay." Her voice sounds shaky. "Go to the library, and next week after . . . you know, things are better, I promise I'll work really hard."

"It's all right," I say. "I can handle it."

Her father says something in the background. "I'd better go, Mel. I'll see you at school."

★ ★ ★

For the whole next week, Dorit's absent, and every night when I call her she can only stay on the phone for five minutes. When I ask how she's doing and if anything's new, her answers are all formal and polite, like I'm a stranger making small talk with her. I hope things will get better once she hears from her grandparents.

I'm back to eating lunch with Lisa and Charlene, the kids who live on my block, because Vicky refuses to pull herself away from Jan and the rest of the Shimmers. Once, she tried to convince me to sit with them, but I almost died. You can't just sit yourself down at the Shimmers' table! I'd feel as out of place as if I showed up in the teachers' lounge with my sandwich.

One day I'm sitting in Girls' Foods, staring at a poster of "The Four Basic Food Groups," when someone knocks at the door. Marla, whom I've only ever seen glued to Shari's side, hands Mrs. Burnes a yellow form.

Mrs. Burnes scowls. "Who in the dickens gave you permission to change classes now?" She sounds flustered, as if letting Marla into Girls' Foods is like adding eggs to her prized soufflé at the wrong time. She ticks her finger up and down the rows of desks and counts us. "I'll have to pair you up with someone experienced."

My heart leaps, and before I overthink it, up shoots my arm. "She can work with me." I have no idea how

I summon the nerve, and I sure as heck can't look at her, because she's *Marla*. She's so much more than I am. But Mrs. Burnes smiles as if I just saved her precious soufflé from caving in. Next thing I know, Marla's sliding into the empty seat next to me.

"Splendid!" Mrs. Burnes says. "Melanie's an expert. She'll bring you up to speed in no time."

My cheeks flame. She makes it sound like we're flying bombers into enemy territory and I'm training Marla to use the navigation system. I only need to show her where measuring cups are and how to turn the oven on. Still, we're paired up for the whole semester. I can't believe it.

"Isn't it funny her name is Mrs. *Burnes* and she teaches cooking?" Marla whispers to me with a lilt in her voice.

I nod fast so I don't get in trouble for talking, but I know I need to relax. This is a big chance for me.

"Does the back of my hair look okay?" Marla whispers. She reaches up and feels around as if something's stuck to her head. "Shari French braided it."

"Yeah, it . . . it looks great." I'd never tell her even if her hair did look bad. Not when she's actually talking to me.

Mrs. Burnes's back is turned, and she's scrawling the words *Vital Nutrients* onto the blackboard.

Marla gives me a once-over like she wants to make sure she has the right person. "Wait—you're friends with Vicky, right?"

"Yeah, like ever since we were born." I try to act cool and casual, but all I'm thinking is, *Marla is talking to me.*

Mrs. Burnes launches into a speech she's probably given for the last twenty years about the miracle of riboflavin.

Marla opens her notebook, and I assume she's going to take notes, but she goes straight for a page filled with Shimmers' names written in bubble letters. *My Bat Mitzvah List* is scribbled at the top. She's drawing stars all around the date: November 17. The usual names are there: Shari, Jan, Jerry, and Aaron Andrews, along with all the others who sit at the middle table at lunch. But then there's Vicky's name, crossed out, and rewritten again in a different color ink at the bottom of the list with a question mark next to it.

Wow. Vicky may not be invited. She already showed me what outfit she's going to wear. Should I tell her? She might be grateful for the heads-up, but she could also be mad at me for knowing something so big before she does.

"Hey!" says Marla, her head snapping in my direction.

I startle. I'm dead if she saw me snooping in her notebook. "I'm—I—"

She points to the eight outfitted mini-kitchens on the other side of the room. "Aren't we supposed to cook in here?"

Relief floods me. "We're still doing nutrition education and kitchen safety," I say, all stiff and professional, like I should be holding a clipboard and wearing a white lab coat.

"You mean it's cooking class but we're not cooking?" she asks, giggling.

I shrug, wishing I had something clever to say but also wanting to stay focused on the *Functions of Riboflavin* chart. If Mrs. Burnes calls on me and I can't answer her question, she'll know I haven't been listening.

"Why're you so red?" Marla asks.

"I . . . it's hot in here." I fan myself.

Really, Melanie? I must do better. This might be my chance.

When Dorit returns to school at the beginning of the next week, I don't mean to pounce, but I haven't heard from her in days. It's like she disappeared.

"You're back!" I say. "God, I've missed you. Did you talk to your grandparents?"

She sets her lunch bag down on our table. Her answer's fast and flat. "Yeah."

"And?"

"They didn't call because they couldn't leave the bomb shelter in their apartment building."

"So—you mean they're okay? Everyone's all right?"

She picks at the straw in her milk carton. "*They* sound okay," she says. "It's my parents who are freaking out. They hate being so far away." From the way her eyes grow glassy, I know I shouldn't push her to explain, but I'm disappointed. I figured she'd want to tell me more. This is the stuff we get about each other. I mean, she must be scared. When Dad and I watched the news last night, the reporters said fighting could go on for weeks, and Israel has lost lots of soldiers.

I offer her a drop biscuit that I baked last night, but she pushes it away.

"You want to sleep over this weekend?" I ask.

"I'm babysitting."

"Is there anything I can do? Do you want to talk?"

She's about to answer when a gaggle of Shimmers, led by Shari, tromps past our table. Someone bumps my chair, and I look up.

"Hi," says Marla. I check behind me to see who she's talking to, but it's *me*. "See ya, *not* in the kitchen." She giggles as her cat eyes meet mine. My insides swell, and I try to hide my smile from Dorit. It's the first time a Shimmer has ever noticed me.

Dorit doesn't miss it. "Wow," she says as soon as the Shimmers have walked away. "You must be on cloud nine."

I shrug, trying to keep my cool. "We're partners in Girls' Foods. It's no big deal." Maybe I should hide how *I* feel too.

Later in the week, we finish the final unit of kitchen practices, "Knives and Their Uses," and Mrs. Burnes finally lets us cook. The room clangs as kids rifle through cabinets for measuring spoons and bowls.

Marla's decked out in her checkered apron, hairnet, and plastic gloves. She looks exactly like everyone else in class—not at all like a Shimmer. "We didn't wear this much protection when we used an electric saw in Girls' Shop last year!"

"Mrs. Burnes said she'll take points off for 'unsafe kitchen practices' if we don't put it all on." I sound like I'm the safety captain of Ashford Junior High.

Marla bumps me with her hip. "We're making cinnamon toast, you turkey—not an atom bomb!" Her eyes are twinkly and happy, like she's ready to have fun. When she comes back from the pantry carrying a canister of sugar, she giggles. "Good thing I have my gloves on. This sugar is toxic!"

I don't want to get in trouble or have Mrs. Burnes think I'm fooling around, but it's funny. I picture us in Dad's lab, pouring sugar into a test tube. When I tell her, she cracks up.

"Stand back!" says Marla. "I'm adding the cinnamon now!"

I hold up a knife. "Take cover! I'm spreading the butter!" We end up laughing so hard, I forget how tongue-tied I usually feel around the Shimmers. And in the end, we make four picture-perfect slices of cinnamon toast.

Mrs. Burnes gathers everyone around our station to see our masterpieces. "This is how it's done, ladies."

After we wipe down our counter and wash our dishes, I wave to Marla on my way out of the classroom. She makes an explosion with her hands, sending us both into giggles. I'm joking with Marla, and it's easy.

Yep, *that's* how it's done.

On Halloween, kids come to school all dressed up. Shari and Marla are twin aliens, wearing matching green shirts and bathing caps covered in aluminum foil, complete with antennas. Even Mr. Pitkewicz gets into the act with his rubber President Nixon mask. Tonight I'll be passing out candy to trick-or-treaters at our house. Ever since junior high started, it feels baby-ish to go out asking for candy. But later I'll meet the neighborhood kids in front of Lisa's house, and we'll share whatever's left over at home.

I'm sitting on my island in the middle of the Sea of Shimmers, and The Pits is teaching us about alliances, explaining how sometimes countries stick together because they *need* one another, not because they're so buddy-buddy. Like, the United States and Russia were on the same side during World War I, but now, in 1973, we're basically mortal enemies. When Mr. Pitkewicz tells us that alliances between countries shift with the times, Marla's bat mitzvah list pops into my head.

The Shimmers have their desks scooted together, and they're passing notes back and forth. My ears twitch when I hear *bat mitzvah invitation*. And there's more: *Live band. Country club.* By the way they're talking about their carpools to the party, I can tell they got their invitations a while ago.

My heart thumps hard. Part of me imagines being invited. A bigger part of me wonders who I'd even talk to or what I'd do if someone asked me to dance. Thinking about it makes my armpits sweat.

Vicky overhears the chatter too. She looks gut-punched, from her sparkly top hat and magician's cape down to her fishnet stockings. "What the heck?" she mouths to me. I don't want to be the one to break the bad news to her, but I feel like I should tell her *something*. I scribble a note and pass it to her when The Pits isn't looking.

I saw your name on the list in Marla's notebook. Maybe her parents made her cut it down?

Across the room, Dorit's hunched over her notebook, scribbling down everything The Pits says. Something's wrong. She avoids talking about herself or her family when we eat lunch, and it's not just because she's worried about her grandparents. The closeness that grew between us all summer has withered away. I want to tell her that whatever's going on with her, I'm here to listen, but she's as hard to get to as one of President Nixon's secret tapes.

When the bell rings, everyone rushes for the doorway. Dorit's squished on one side of me, Vicky on the other, and the Shimmers in front. World War I alliances? Mr. Pitkewicz should check out eighth grade.

"Cute costume," says Vicky, pointing to Marla's antennas.

"Thanks." She barely turns around.

I see the wheels spinning in Vicky's head as she schemes for Marla to notice her. "I look like an alien every day. My clothes are the worst." She turns to me and says loudly, "Hey, Mel, let's ditch school on Monday and buy new outfits at the mall."

Dorit rolls her eyes.

"Vicky, I'm not skipping school—"

She tugs at my arm. "Mel, I'm joking! No school on Monday. Teachers' in-service."

My face warms. "Oh . . ."

"Calm down, Miss Gullible. I wouldn't dream of breaking rules with *you*."

On Friday, instead of lecturing us about the wonders of thiamine, Mrs. Burnes hands out papers with *Kitchen Scavenger Hunt* printed at the top.

"A little fun today! Remember, no school Monday, so let's give it our all." She shoos us to our stations, pointing to cabinets and drawers. "Some of you still don't know the difference between a griddle and a skillet, but after this little activity you will. Good luck!"

Our sheet is divided into twelve squares, with a clue or a question about a kitchen tool in each one. I read the first clue. "*I can't help when your windshield is covered in ice, but use me to get every last drop of cake batter from your bowl.*"

"Huh?" says Marla. "That makes no sense."

We make a few bad guesses before we finally figure it out.

"Oh," says Marla. "I've got it! It's a rubber scraper. You know, like *scraping* ice?" We open the drawer under our counter, pluck it out by its plastic handle, and show it to Mrs. Burnes, who initials the square on our paper.

Her clues are tricky, but eventually we find the teaspoons and tablespoons, the wooden spoons, the stockpots, the saucepans, even the pastry blender and the wide spatula. When we solve the last square's clue for a garlic press, we slap hands up high and yell "Yes!"

While everyone else is still scrambling to solve clues, we sit down on the floor, backs leaned against our stove.

"You have gym yet?" asks Marla. "Miss Becker made us run outside. My legs are *killing* me."

Mrs. Burnes claps her hands together. "Think, people: how many pieces are there to a *double boiler?*"

A collective "*Oh . . .*" echoes through the classroom.

"Hey," whispers Marla, pulling over her book bag. "Do you go to Hebrew school?"

My stomach flips. Maybe I'm about to get an invitation! "Um, I quit after one year. But I feel awful now that I didn't stay and have a bat mitzvah. They're so much fun. I love going to them."

She unzips a side pocket and digs around inside. I'm dreaming she'll pull out an envelope. "Well, according to my rabbi, it doesn't matter whether you go to Hebrew school or have a big party or do *anything*. He says you become a bat or bar mitzvah automatically when you turn thirteen. He's big into teaching us that every Jewish person is as Jewish as the next."

My eyes don't leave her hand as she roots around in another zipper compartment.

"Anyway," she says, "I have something cool for you."

I ready myself for a fancy invitation with my name on it. Instead, she drops a piece of bubble gum into my hand. It's shiny red, shaped like a mini hot dog. "It's from this place next to *my* boring Hebrew school, Leon's Deli. They sell all these neat kinds of gum and candy."

I feel like I got tripped while running. Why did I think someone like Marla would invite me to her bat mitzvah? We cook together in this class because I volunteered to help her, not because we're actually friends. The plastic wrapper crinkles as I stuff it deep into my jeans pocket. No way am I getting kicked out of class for chewing a ridiculous piece of hot dog gum.

"Thanks. I—I'll save it for later." I pray my eyes don't start tearing up.

Marla gives me a funny look. "Maybe you shouldn't dress so warm. You're turning bright red again."

Mrs. Burnes calls, "Time's up!" and collects the papers. She smiles wide at ours and hands Marla and me colored pencils that say *Now You're Cooking!* "Nice work, ladies—you're the only ones with a hundred percent."

The bell sounds, and Marla saunters off with a wave. I clutch the pencil in one hand, feel the gum wrapper in my pocket with the other. If I were six years old, today would've felt like an amazing prize-filled day.

But I'm thirteen, and junior high isn't a carnival.

Chapter 12

OVER THE WEEKEND, I HOP INTO THE CAR WITH Dad for his Sunday morning shopping run to Buck's Hardware. I'm buying copper wire and washers to make a bracelet I saw in an old *Teen Beat*. Plus Buck's sells the yummiest caramels at the checkout.

"What do you need today?" I ask Dad.

"A sandbag and a new snow brush for Mom's car. Winter's coming."

We wait at a red light. He can buy them, but she won't drive. Slippery roads still scare her. Snow? Sleet? Ice? Forget it. *Won't* isn't even the right word—she *can't*. Asking her for a ride when the weather's not picture-perfect is like asking someone to stand out on a window ledge at the top of a skyscraper.

Two years ago, snow came early, around Halloween. I missed a lot then: sleepovers, birthday parties. She even kept me home from school on blustery days because she didn't trust the bus driver.

We turn at the corner. Ashford Avenue is quiet this

morning. Dad's favorite radio station—the all-news one—buzzes as we glide down the empty street. When the announcer mentions Watergate, Dad raises the volume.

. . . the most serious constitutional crisis in American history. Last night the president fired the Watergate special prosecutor . . . stunning development . . . nothing like it ever happened before . . .

"Unbelievable," says Dad. The light turns green.

"What?" I ask.

"Nixon still won't hand over his tapes, even though the Supreme Court ordered him to. Now he's fired the person in charge of the investigation."

"He can't do that, can he?"

Dad sighs. He's not like Jon, who'll call the president a liar and a crook and spout off his opinion. Dad's a scientist who carefully considers the evidence before he reaches conclusions. "I'll tell you this," he says, stepping on the gas. "Something *bad* must be on those secret tapes of his if he won't let the investigators hear them."

"Doesn't he realize hiding them makes him look guiltier?" It's like the time Jerry Finkel wrote a bunch of spelling words on his hand before a test. At the end of class, Mrs. Monticello—aka The Monster—asked to see him, but instead of staying, he ran out and washed the words off in the boys' bathroom. She gave him an F.

We rumble into the parking lot. "People do all sorts of things when they're desperate," Dad says. "You'd be surprised how they panic when they're backed against a wall."

Inside Buck's Hardware, Dad heads to the "Just Arrived" section where bags of salt are piled and shovels hang from hooks. As I search for the aisle with the washers, a table with last season's merchandise catches my eye. Picked-over pool toys and open packs of rubber rings—like the ones Dorit and I dived for—are marked down to fifty percent off. Loneliness stabs at me. Lately, we've barely talked about anything except our social studies project.

Down an aisle, I open little drawers and check out the bazillions of different-sized washers. I pick a bunch for my bracelet and drop them into a small paper bag.

On my way back to the front of the store, I notice a "Home Security" display. Some guy's piling door latches and bolts into a basket. He's asking Mr. Buckman why the store doesn't sell stronger locks.

"You really don't need steel-grade locks to keep your house safe," Mr. Buckman tells him.

"How you sure my house is safe?" says the man in a familiar Israeli accent.

I look over. It's Dorit's father.

I want to wave, but he's scowling, and I figure it's not the best time to say hi. Instead, I turn down the closest aisle, which is full of stacked paint cans, and find myself face-to-face with Dorit.

"Melanie!" She looks happy to see me, but her eyes quickly dart toward her father. "We're . . . picking up stuff for our house." Her lip has that little tremble as she forces a smile. "Some better locks."

"Did someone break into your house?"

"No! It's just, ever since the war in Israel started, he worries . . . about protecting our family." Her voice is so tight, like a million words are straining to tumble out but she won't let them. Not here in the middle of Buck's Hardware.

I don't know what to say. When I reach out to her, she stiffens. "Dorit, did I do something to make you mad?" I blurt out. "You hardly talk to me about anything besides school anymore."

She lets out a sigh, but her expression doesn't change. "Melanie, there's stuff that's too hard to explain. My parents are worried about our family in Israel. And they feel guilty that they're not there helping or something."

"But why can't we talk about it? We're . . . I thought we were best friends."

"Dorit!" Her father motions to the checkout.

"I'd better go. See you at school."

★ ★ ★

Ten fifteen, Monday morning. I poke around my jacket pocket to check if my change is still there.

"I don't like the look of those clouds," Mom says, peering out the window. "You should stay home."

My heart pounds. She's not going to ruin my day. "The weather's fine."

"But you've never taken a public bus before. Where'd you get such an idea?"

"Dad said I could."

"Why can't Vicky's parents drive you?"

"They have plans." It's about to spiral; *she's* about to spiral. I can feel it. "I'm going. I asked Dad, and he said I could." I hate talking to her like this—it feels so mean. But Jon told me if I don't, she'll make me scared of everything.

"You'll need extra cash." She heads to the table where her purse usually sits. "Just in case . . ."

Just in case the bus breaks down.

Just in case someone kidnaps me and I need ransom.

Just in case there's a sudden blizzard and I need to hire a team of sled dogs to bring me home.

Mom rifles through a pile of Jon's old newspapers, knocking a stack of mail to the floor. "Where's my purse?" she asks, her voice rising. "I always keep it over here."

I bend to pick up the assortment of bills and magazines. "It's here, under the table." As I drop the mail back into the basket, a cream-colored envelope addressed to "Miss Melanie Adler" pokes out. "Hang on. Why didn't you give me this?"

"Oh! It came on Saturday. I forgot all about it." She shoves a five-dollar bill at me and launches into her dire warnings about strangers and bus drivers and creeps at the mall, but I'm tearing open the smooth paper, pulling out a pink card with a Jewish star and raised lettering.

It is with great happiness that we invite you
to join us as our daughter
MARLA RENEE FORSTEIN
becomes a bat mitzvah

My hands are shaking. She invited me! Saturday, November 17, 1973. That's next week!

She invited me last-minute. Not like everyone else. The pang of that disappointment only lasts for a second, though.

Bat mitzvah presentation followed by dinner and dancing
Highland Hills Country Club
7 pm

A fancy party with the Shimmers!

"Hey, anybody home?" Vicky's voice sounds on the other side of the screen door.

I stuff the envelope into my pocket before she can see. The page of Marla's notebook with her bat mitzvah list flashes before my eyes. I wonder if she got a last-minute invitation too, or if she hasn't been invited at all. I'm not sure I should bring it up.

"I'll be home by three," I tell Mom, leaping for the door. "Before it gets dark." And more softly, "I promise, Mommy."

One look at Vicky's fluffy hair and glossy face tells me why she's late.

"Took you long enough," I say, already heading toward the bus stop.

"Sorry. I couldn't find my purse."

"You too?"

"Huh?"

"Oh, nothing. My mom lost hers this morning." A few months ago, I would've told her the whole back-and-forth between me and Mom, but not anymore. It always bugged me when Vicky joked about Mom's worries, and now I understand why—they're real, and they're not funny. Dorit understood that. I miss her.

I run my fingers along Vicky's faded denim bag

made from an old pair of jeans. "You can't go any-where without your suitcase, can you?"

"Comes in handy. What do you need? A chocolate kiss? Mascara? I have everything."

A rumbling engine sounds up ahead.

"Oh, shoot," I say. "The express—here it comes!"

"Let's run!"

We make it to the corner just in time to scramble onto the bus.

The window is cool against my cheek. We rumble past Buck's Hardware and The Scoop. There's a banner in front of the JCC: *Hanukkah Carnival—Sunday, December 16.*

A man behind me rattles his newspaper. "Can you believe this?" He nudges the lady next to him and reads out loud. "*Should President Nixon Go? Congress to Consider Impeachment.*" I don't have to be Jon to know that sounds serious.

"You're awfully quiet," says Vicky. She's looking at me with pity. I curl my fingers around the invitation folded up in my pocket. No one needs to feel sorry for me. This is going to be my year.

We get off the bus in front of Katt and Company, Mom's favorite department store. The smell of roasted nuts wafts over from the candy counter as we burst through the doorway. Heels clatter on linoleum, and shoppers bustle past. Someone carrying a stack of boxes bumps into me.

"Let's hit Cosmetics first," I say, pushing a row of hanging neckties out of my way. Today I'm in charge; I'm not letting Vicky drag me around to every place she wants to go. "I hope they have the cool lip gloss I saw on TV."

A display of perfume bottles stands on the front counter. "Midnight Blue. I love this." Before spraying it, I peer through the slender bottle made of deep blue glass.

"C'm'ere, farm girl," Vicky singsongs.

"What did you say?"

"Don't you remember that 'What's Your Scent?' quiz we took in *Teen Beat*? You're a Farm Girl!"

I actually scored highest for "Nature Girl"—outdoorsy scents like flowers, woods, and wind. Right away, Vicky nicknamed me Farm Girl. It's not funny, and it never was.

"Cut it out. There's nothing wrong with liking nature scents."

Vicky makes a face and sprays me with a burst of Spring Meadows, not much different than the lotion I used for poison ivy last summer. Yikes. I hope I don't smell like a medicine cabinet all day.

"Here's the stuff I saw on TV," I say. "Luscious Lip Treats."

She holds a tube of the gloss to her nose. "Mmm! Strawberry."

I paw through the bin and hand her another. "Look, this one's Bubblegum—and here's Raspberry Parfait and Cherries Jubilee." I try Bananas 'n' Cream. "Yum." I turn it over to check the price: $2.50. "Should I buy it?"

Vicky glances behind me. "Hold on, Farm Girl," she whispers. "I'll get it for you—my treat." Reaching up with one hand, she grabs a tin of bath powder off a high shelf. With her other hand, she slips two tubes of Luscious Lip Treats into her denim bag. "One for you, and one for me."

"Vicky, what do you think you're doing?"

"Take it easy. We did this all summer in California, and I never got caught. Not once."

The sales clerk hangs up the phone and heads toward us. She stares us up and down, her eyes zeroing in on Vicky's oversized purse. "Can I help you ladies?"

That's it. I'm going to get arrested right here.

"Uh, no . . . we're just looking." My voice shakes. Rivers of sweat run beneath my jacket.

"Ask me next time you want something off a high shelf. Don't try and grab it by yourself." She teeters on spiky heels back to her stool. "Coulda had powder flying all over the place!"

I yank Vicky across the aisle next to a rack of ponchos. A lump chokes my throat. I try not to lose my cool.

"Vicky, my parents will kill me if I get caught shoplifting. Besides, it's *wrong*."

"You're acting like we're armed robbers. They're not gonna miss two little tubes of lip gloss." She grabs my sleeve. "You want to hang out with the cool kids? Try doing something cool for once in your life. Shari does it. She calls it the five-finger discount."

"Why do you think you know so much about being cool?"

She snorts. "What would you rather do—sit at Dorit's house and look at her stamp collection?"

She tries to link her arm through mine, but I pull away, my blood boiling. "If you're so cool, how come you're not invited to Marla's bat mitzvah?" After the last word leaves my mouth, I feel like I just threw up all over her.

She freezes. "How do you know I'm not invited?"

"I . . . I just do." I didn't even know for sure until this moment. Marla really didn't invite her. Wow.

"Wait," she says. "*You're* invited?"

Now I feel like my puke's all over the floor and I'm stuck cleaning it up. "I am."

"Are you going?"

"If I'm not in jail for shoplifting."

She rolls her eyes, but she doesn't have a comeback this time. After looking over her shoulder to make sure no sales clerks are around, she pulls the two pink tubes from her bag and slides them onto a shelf.

I nod approvingly. "Let's get out of here before that sales lady comes back."

I've had two firsts in one day: a Shimmer invited me to her bat mitzvah party, *and* Vicky listened to me for once. Maybe now I'm the one taking steps away from her, instead of the other way around, and it doesn't make me sad. It makes me feel strong.

Chapter 13

ON TUESDAY, MARLA'S WAITING AT OUR KITCHEN station. "Did you get it?"

I put on my best puzzled face, trying to play it cool. "Get what?"

"My bat mitzvah invitation, you dork! I sent you one!"

"Oh, yeah," I say, like I'm just remembering. "Thanks. I think I can make it."

Marla must see right through me because she smiles. "Sorry about messing with you last week," she says, elbowing me. "But you should've seen your face when I handed you a piece of bubble gum instead of an invitation—it was hilarious!" She doesn't mention that she mailed mine way after everyone else's, and I don't ask her about that. For all I know, she only did it as an act of charity, a good deed. I hope not, but either way I feel lucky; I could've been shut out like Vicky. "Well, I can't wait," I say.

Marla watches me like she expects me to say more.

But I obviously can't tell her that I've been waiting for this day since sixth grade, that I won't sleep for the next week, that I only have a week to find the perfect outfit, and that I pray that I'll be able to relax and have fun instead of worrying what everyone at the party thinks of me. She has no idea that I'm more nervous for her bat mitzvah than *she* is.

Every day for the next week, as soon as I get home from school I plant myself in front of my closet: pulling out dresses, holding them up, trying them on, and dreaming about Saturday night. I take down my maxi dress from Rosh Hashanah. The oversized collar and patchwork-patterned bottom look old-fashioned and droopy. And there's a stain from where I dripped grape juice on the sleeve. I don't own one piece of clothing that'll make me look like I belong at this bat mitzvah with the Shimmers.

I tote the dress down the hall, hanger and all, to show Mom. I'm planning to ask—no, to beg—her to take me to buy something new tomorrow. Before I get the chance, the phone rings.

"Melanie!" Mom calls from the kitchen, "it's for you!" When she hands me the receiver she whispers, "It sounds like Dorit."

"Hey," says the voice at the other end. It *is* Dorit.

"Hi!" I glance at Mom, who's trying to look busy

at the sink, but the tilt of her head tells me she's listening hard. I stretch the coiled phone cord as far as it will go down the basement stairs. "How are you? I can't believe you're calling!"

"Our phone's free again. Finally."

"Everyone's okay?" I don't expect her to tell me details, but I wish she would.

"Yeah," she says. "My grandparents are staying at my aunt and uncle's apartment in Tel Aviv. And they said the fighting is ending. Israel won the war—at least for now." She doesn't sound as relieved as I expect her to.

"That's good—right?"

She lets out a laugh, but she doesn't sound amused. "It's better than being at war." There's an edge to her voice I've only heard her use with people she doesn't like. "I called because I want to know if you can sleep over. I already asked my parents."

Happiness balloons in my chest. Finally! We'll play a marathon Scrabble game and raid her refrigerator while everyone's asleep. I won't even mind if her little brothers hang around. And maybe she'll tell me more about what's been worrying her instead of keeping it bottled up like she does lately. "For sure," I say. "That sounds awesome."

She lets out a massive sigh, like when she gets a test back that she's sure she bombed—even though she always ends up with the highest grade in the class. "I haven't gone anywhere or done anything in weeks. I'm going nuts, being the official babysitter."

"Well, name the day. I'll be there." I'm not even thinking, and I should be.

"This Saturday night. And maybe you could eat dinner here too."

This Saturday night?

My mouth suddenly feels cottony. I haven't told her about Marla's bat mitzvah yet. It's not that I've purposely been keeping it a secret from her—it shouldn't even be such a big deal between us. But it is. She will always think the Shimmers are a bunch of show-offs who are full of themselves, and she'll never understand why I want to be one.

"Are you still there?"

"Yeah." I try to clear the glob of goop growing in my throat. "Do you think we could do it on Friday night instead?" I say it quietly so Mom can't hear. "I think I have to go somewhere with my parents on Saturday." If Jon were listening he'd say I'm using my "lying voice." I hope Dorit can't tell.

"I guess that's okay," she says.

"Great! After I get home on Friday, I'll pack my overnight bag and come straight over. You won't have to spend another minute alone with your brothers!"

But by Thursday, my plans unravel like the fringe on my cutoff shorts.

Snow. The weather forecasters totally miss it, and even though it's not a blizzard, it's more than a few flakes. "It's looking horrible out there," Mom says, pulling me into a hug in front of our house after school. "I was starting to wonder why you weren't home yet."

That rubs at me the wrong way because I know she wasn't just *wondering*—she's been craning her neck, looking out for me, for the past half hour.

"What's the big deal?" I shake her off me. "Wow, it's snowing in November."

"This is more than a little snow. I'm going to call Dad and tell him to leave work now before he gets stuck there overnight."

As she picks up the phone I want to shout, *Look at how pretty it is! Some people are happy! They're going to build snowmen and jump on their sleds and have fun!*

Instead I say, "I guess we're not going shopping to buy an outfit for Marla's bat mitzvah."

"If this keeps up, you won't be going to any bat mitzvah."

All at once, the excitement that's carried me around the whole week plunges like a snapped cable car, plummeting until it hits the ground. I'm not missing Marla's bat mitzvah because of a few snowflakes.

"That's not fair!" I choke out. "Do you even know how important this is to me? You're not keeping me home. Dad promised he'd drive me."

Jon comes out of his room. "Don't worry, Mom." He puts his arm around her. "It's supposed to clear up overnight, and they're saying by tomorrow it'll all melt away."

He's trying to calm her down, but she's busy on the phone, telling Dad to drive home slowly. When she gets like this, reasoning with her is like talking to an empty room. If I look closely enough, I can almost see her heart pounding.

The next evening, even though Jon swore it was going to stop, big flakes whirl past our living room window as Dad helps me zip my overnight bag.

Mom doesn't say, "What an exciting weekend you have planned" or "I'm so happy you and Dorit are getting together again." Instead, she looks at Dad and sighs as if he's betrayed her.

He jingles his car keys, like he's set on keeping the tone nice and light. "The salt truck just passed by, and we're only driving four blocks to her best friend's house. No need to catastrophize this one."

I'm so relieved that Dad understands, that he wants me to be happy and sticks up for me.

"Salt truck? Look how fast it's coming down,"

Mom says. "What if the Shoshanis decide to take her somewhere? They don't know how to drive in this—they're from Israel!"

My throat tightens. "Dad? Can we please go?"

But he just stands here looking back and forth, first at Mom, and then at me. He's letting her get to him after all.

"Jon!" I call without thinking. "Will you walk me to Dorit's house?"

I don't know how he hears me over the thumping of his stereo, but a minute later he's in the living room, throwing on his parka and a pair of boots. "Come on," he says. "Let's get out of here." Mom and Dad stand speechless as he pulls me out the front door without giving them a chance to protest.

"Did you hear everything?" I ask him as we walk down the hill.

"Yeah, not that I'm surprised. It happens at least once every winter."

"I . . . I'm sorry. I didn't mean for you to spend your Friday night being my chaperone." The wind blows a spray of snow off a tree and into my face.

"It's okay. This summer, when I get my license, I'll be able to drive you anywhere." We crunch down the sidewalk, letting that sink in. I wonder if Mom will even let him learn to drive.

"What if they won't let me go to Marla's bat mitz-vah?" I say, my mind racing to tomorrow night.

"Don't worry," Jon says. "You won't miss it—even if I have to take you there by piggyback!"

Something about the way he says it makes me giggle, and I give him a hug. He can sure be a pain sometimes, but tonight he's my rock.

At the Shoshanis' house, Jon stands back and waves when the door opens.

"Come on in," Dorit says in a hushed voice. "Give me your bag—you look frozen."

"Jon walked me over here," I say, clomping in like I usually do. "My mom refuses to drive in the snow, and at the last minute she decided she wouldn't let my dad drive either." I want to blab out the whole awful scene to her, but she interrupts me.

"Put your boots over here on the mat while I grab my puffer." She says it in an almost-whisper. "My asthma's horrible today." She bustles me toward the far wall of the living room, like she doesn't want me to see something—but not fast enough. Her father shuffles past wearing a ratty robe and socks, his hair all messy. Dorit's eyes dart away.

Mrs. Shoshani is huddled in the corner of the living room, talking on the telephone in hushed Hebrew. She doesn't say hello to me—doesn't even seem to notice me. Unlit Shabbat candles sit in silver holders, like someone forgot about them.

Benny and Natan bound down the hall and leap at me. "What took you so long? Dorit promised you'd play War with us. Why don't you ever come here anymore?"

"Sorry—they've been waiting for you since school let out." Dorit slides her inhaler off the bookshelf.

I wrap my fingers around the deck of cards the boys shove into my hands. It's weird how she wants me to play with them when usually she's trying to get them out of our hair. Last time I was here, she threatened to call Animal Control when they wouldn't leave us alone. We had a good laugh about that. I ease down to the rug and shuffle the cards.

"How do you do that?" Benny asks as they cascade into a pile.

"My Grandpa Jack taught me—isn't it cool?"

"I'm going to heat up our dinner," Dorit says, leaving the three of us. "Don't make too much noise." Everything feels strange. She's barely talking, and when she does, it's in short sentences, telling everybody what to do.

After our bazillionth game of War, Benny says, "Ema, I'm starving."

Mrs. Shoshani covers the telephone receiver with her hand and calls, "Dorit!"

In an instant, she pops out of the kitchen. "Are

you done playing already? Then come on in—dinner's ready." She tries to soften her tone so her brothers don't completely lose their smiles.

"Here, let me help you." I pull dishes from the cluttered cabinet as the boys slip into their seats. Dorit hands me a bowl of salad, and she carries a platter of rice and vegetables to the table. Her brothers look sullen, chewing slowly. The refrigerator hums, distracting in the silence. "Mm," I say, trying to lighten things up. "This tastes really good."

"Don't be too impressed—my mom made it this afternoon when she came home from work," says Dorit. "All I did was heat it up."

Mrs. Shoshani comes into the kitchen, untangling the long cord as she speaks clearly into the telephone.

"Mulberry Street. *M-u-l-b-e-r-r-y.* Cain. Shalom, Estie. Bye." She hangs the receiver up on the wall.

"Ema, who's coming over?" asks Benny.

"Some very old friends of ours, Amnon and Estie Roth. Tomorrow night. They're visiting from Israel for this whole year." She doesn't sit down to eat. Instead, she disappears down the hall and clicks her bedroom door closed.

Benny lets out a loud burp, and he and Natan both crack up. Natan's elbow knocks over his glass. "Oh no! My water!"

"You made a meh-ess!" sings Benny.

"Shhhhh!" Dorit hisses. "Stop the noise! Abba is resting!"

I notice their wounded faces. I dash from my seat and grab paper towels. "Don't worry, guys. I spill stuff all the time."

After dinner and cleanup, the boys head to their room, and Dorit and I retreat to hers. Dorit and I put on pajamas and lounge on her bed with a pile of *National Geographic* magazines. I flip through pictures: a herd of cattle, ancient cave paintings, the Amazon River.

The house is still—only the crinkle of magazine pages and Dorit's wheezy coughs.

"Thanks for sleeping over tonight. If I had to spend another Friday night with just my brothers, I think I'd jump out my window." She doesn't look up from the picture of snow geese flying in front of the moon.

"Yeah, that would be awful," I say, "especially since your room's on the ground floor." I'm glad she laughs. "I'm happy you called me. It feels weird that we barely see each other lately. I guess you're always busy watching them."

"Believe me, it's not by choice." I've never seen her cry before, but her trembly lip makes me sit up.

"Dorit, can you tell me what else is wrong?"

"Nothing."

She answers in a snap, squashing the question like it's a spider creeping across her floor. When she hands me another pile of magazines, I guess it means I should stop asking.

It makes me think about our first sleepover and how it felt scary to talk at the beginning. We hardly even knew each other last spring, but we could tell right away we had something big in common. And once I started opening up about Mom, and Dorit told me about her father, something clicked. I fell asleep happy that night, knowing that someone finally understood me. I felt a lot less alone. I know she did too.

And last summer, when Mom freaked out every time I wanted to swim or ride my bike to her house, for the first time ever, I didn't try to hide it. Each time, Dorit treated it as a fact of life we'd deal with—and we did.

I never expected that after all this time, she'd keep important things from me. I'm sleeping here tonight, but it doesn't feel like a sleepover. And all at once it really starts to get to me.

"I know something's not right," I say. "And I can't force you to talk about it, but maybe you'd feel better if you did. I mean, with the way things are with my family, you know I'll understand."

She pushes her magazines to the floor and takes

her time smoothing out her blanket, like she's deciding whether to say anything. The alarm clock on her dresser ticks so loudly. "It's almost impossible for you to understand. I mean, you're not Israeli. Not that I really am either, but my parents were born there, and when something bad happens, it hits them really hard. My father especially."

She flicks at a thread on her blanket.

"It's weird: he feels guilty that he's not there defending Israel, but he's also so freaked out by loud noises and soldiers and all of that because of what happened to him in the Six-Day War. It's like he's not sure he could fight even if he *were* there. And it's eating him up. It makes us so . . ." Her voice weakens and she swipes at her eyes.

"I'm really sorry." I don't have anything smart to say to make her feel better, any more than she would have the magic words for me when Mom is going bonkers. I hate that I can't do something to help her.

"I think I'm ready to turn out the light." She straightens the pile of magazines on the floor. "Is that okay?"

I slide off her bed and land on the trundle. "Sure. Unless you want to get a snack or make safety pin necklaces. I brought my beads."

She must hear the disappointment in my voice.

"I . . . I didn't realize how tired I am," she says, taking a shot from her puffer. "Stay up and read if you want. Turn the light off when you're ready."

When she fluffs out her blanket and curls up in bed, I lie down with a nature magazine that has a pair of hikers on its cover. Inside, there's a picture of a polar bear standing all alone on a hunk of ice that's floating in the ocean. Tonight that's how I feel—lonely, drifting.

In the middle of the night, Dorit's breathing turns loud and wheezy, and it wakes me up. Her room's pitch black, and no matter how much I flip my pillow or rearrange my blankets, I can't fall back to sleep. I grope along the wall to feel my way to the bathroom for a drink. I'm pretty sure it's across the hall, but in the darkness, I'm mixed up, and I land in the middle of the stale-smelling living room. The fuzzy outline of someone sitting on the sofa startles me.

Mr. Shoshani.

Goose bumps prickle my arms. The tip of his cigarette glows orange.

On tiptoes, I creep away, trying not to creak the wood floor, trying to disappear before he sees me barging in on him.

Just a few more steps . . .

The hall is so close . . .

I trip over someone's shoes lying on the floor. I stumble into a table, knocking over a pile of books.

Mr. Shoshani shrieks, "Who's there?" He drops down to his hands and knees, and the moonlight catches his terrified face.

I run back to bed and bury myself deep into my covers. I squeeze my eyes closed and imagine walking into Marla's bat mitzvah party. It's the only way I fall asleep.

When I open my eyes in the morning, it's already eight o'clock, and I can hear Dorit scolding her brothers in the kitchen. I quickly slip on my jeans and sweater and stuff my pajamas into my overnight bag. I can't hang around here today—not after what happened last night. Besides, I have a stack of *Teen Beat* magazines waiting to show me how to do my hair and makeup for tonight.

Tonight!

What if no one talks to me and I have to sit alone? What if someone talks to me and I can't think of anything to say? What if Jerry Finkel asks me to dance? I have to go home and think about everything.

As I pass through the living room, Benny's voice drifts out from the kitchen. "Abba, are you up?" When he sees it's only me, his face falls.

"Shh, Benny! Not yet. Come here and I'll fix your breakfast," says Dorit.

"I hope he doesn't stay in bed all day again. I want to *do* something."

Dorit tightens her ponytail. "I'll take you sledding later if he doesn't want to go."

I sit down, and Benny climbs into my lap.

"Mellie, will you come to the sledding hill with us?"

I hug him. "I'm sorry, but I can't. I'm getting ready for a party tonight."

Dorit puts down a bowl of pancake batter and looks at me.

"Marla's bat mitzvah." I don't know why I'm choosing this moment to tell her something that I know will upset her, but I can't help it. I can't hold it in any longer.

Dorit raises her eyebrows. "You're invited to that hotshot convention?" She's heard the Shimmers talking about it in Mr. Pitkewicz's class. Everyone has.

"Marla and I have Girls' Foods together. We're friendly." I don't want to say we're friends because even I know that's not exactly true. I'm still not a hundred percent sure why she invited me.

"Well, have a blast," Dorit says and flips a pancake. I wait for her to tell me all the reasons I shouldn't go or to ask me for the bazillionth time why it's so important to me to be in their stuck-up group, but she only dips a ladle into the bowl and pours a fresh circle of batter onto the griddle.

I can barely believe how mixed-up things have become between us. It's always felt like a relief to be here with Dorit and her family. No matter how weird things got with Mom, I could always count on them to keep me calm. Now I just want to grab my bag and get out of here. I can't stay in a place that feels even more intense than my own house.

Chapter 14

THE SQUEAK OF OUR FRONT DOOR DOESN'T even wake Mom when I get home.

It's so peaceful with everyone still in bed, as if our fighting yesterday never happened.

But it did.

The sun finally pokes through a billowy cloud, and the living room window is cool on my forehead. *Please, God, let Mom have a good day. Let Dad drive me to Marla's bat mitzvah. Let me feel happy and pretty. Let me fit in tonight.*

"Who's up?" Mom's whisper breaks through the silence.

"It's me. I'm home."

"Come in here, sweetie." She sounds calmer than last night.

Her bedroom floor creaks under my stockinged feet. "Hi, Mommy." I lean down to her warmth, to the softness of her blankets.

She doesn't ask how I got home from Dorit's. Her smile is forced and heavy with regret: another awful scene, another night she wishes she could do over. She'll never say it, but I know.

She reaches under her bed and pulls out a cardboard box. "I bought this for you last night, after . . . after you left. Dad drove me. They were about to close, but we talked them into keeping it open for us."

"You went there in the snow?"

"I promised I'd get you a new dress. You've been so excited for tonight . . ." She doesn't finish, and she looks more sad than happy. "I hope it's right."

She slips the box into my hands. I lift the lid and remove the tissue paper. A pink-and-white maxi dress sits inside. I touch the ruffled shoulders—it's exactly what I wanted. If we'd seen it in the store, I would've grabbed it in a second and begged Mom to let me try it on. Holding it up now, I realize she paid a ton of money for it just to show how bad she feels. "Thank you, Mommy," I say. "It's perfect."

By midafternoon, I can't watch the clock anymore, so I kick into high gear. First, a steamy hot shower and a desperate prayer for my hair to turn out. I flip through this month's *Teen Beat* feature: "20 New Hairdos for a New You." Every picture shows girls with straight blond hair, long and parted down the middle. What about people like me who have frizzy hair or dark hair? What about people with dark skin? *Teen Beat* thinks all teenagers look the same. That's why Dorit refuses to read it. She always complains that no one looks that perfect in real life and to even try is wrong. Maybe she's right, but tonight, I can't help it—I'm trying.

For Hanukkah last year, Mom and Dad bought me a new kind of hair dryer called a Super Max. Instead of sitting around wearing a plastic shower cap connected to a contraption that blows hot air in through a hose, you hold the small dryer in your hand. You can style your hair with a brush while you blow it dry—if you know what you're doing. Some people call them blow-dryers. After a lot of poufy-hair days, I've gotten the hang of it.

When the lights from Dad's car flash at me in our driveway, I throw on my coat and hug Mom—who's been quiet all day, probably still feeling bad about our fight. I float outside in my pink dress, careful not to touch my hair or smudge what little mascara I'm allowed to wear.

"You clean up pretty well," Dad teases when I open the car door. As he drives down our block, the streetlights glimmer through my window. Our car isn't a carriage, and I'm not headed to a royal ball, but I feel special. Maybe my life is about to change. Maybe tonight I will become one of the Shimmers.

What will Vicky think? And Dorit?

At Ashford Avenue, Dad slows down. "How do you like that? They're closed—all the gas stations." Signs spray-painted on plywood say *Regular Customers Only, Closed Weekends,* and *Sorry, Out of Gas.*

"Don't we have enough gas?" My stomach lurches.

"I hope so," he says. "Yesterday I waited in line for more than an hour before giving up. And look at the price—sixty-five cents a gallon! Highway robbery! That's almost as bad as that crook in New York, charging ninety-nine cents. Did you see that on the news?"

The Pits explained about it in class this week. A bunch of Arab countries with oil supplies stopped their shipments to the United States. They're mad because we sent weapons to Israel when the war broke out. Now we have a gas shortage. As far as I care, all we need is enough to get me to the party and back.

The red needle hugs the "E" on the fuel gauge as my heart thumps. Finally, we pull around a long circle drive that brings us to the country club's entrance. Two stories of brick and ivy stare me down.

I'm about to go to a party with the Shimmers.

"You want me to walk you in?" Dad asks, opening the car door for me. "Those fancy shoes of yours are going to be awfully slick on that ice."

"No! I'm fine, Dad. I'll be careful. But thanks. I'll call you when I'm ready to come home." I jingle the change for the pay phone so he can hear it.

Inside, it's warm and smells like a mixture of perfume and roast beef. Women in sequined evening gowns and men in suits tower over me. A chandelier sparkles overhead, and I glide across the plush carpeting.

"Let's check your coat, zeeskeit," says a woman with the tiniest bit of an accent. She has short hair—black with flecks of gray—and when she smiles with her green cat-eyes that look just like Marla's, I realize this must be her mom. With her simple navy floor-length dress and only a dab of lipstick, she looks a lot less fancy than I expected.

"I don't know what happened to the girls," she says, leading me to the coat check. "Last time I saw them, they were headed toward the ladies' room." She blows a kiss to someone. "By the way, I'm Marla's mother, in case the resemblance didn't give it away."

"I'm Melanie."

She squints like she's trying to figure out if she knows me.

"Marla and I just became friends."

She grabs my arm. "You're the cook!"

Marla's mentioned me to her mom!

"Uh, yeah," I say. "Only a lot of the stuff we make in Girls' Foods is kind of gross."

She laughs, and then she's off, rushing over to hug some lady with a hairdo that reminds me of cotton candy.

I weave through the crowd, but there's no one my age anywhere—just a bunch of little kids, dressed up and pulling on their parents' arms. Waiters mill around with trays of hors d'oeuvres and glasses of wine. I duck over to the ladies' room and listen before I open the door.

"Who do you think she'll dance with first?"

That's Shari's voice, followed by a chorus of girls hooting, "Aaron Andrews!" and giggling all around.

I grab the door handle. *Here goes nothing.*

Everyone's huddled around mirrors. Marla drops her hairbrush on the counter. "Melanie! You made it!" When no one turns around, she pulls me over. "Guys, this is Melanie. She's my cooking partner!"

"You haven't burned down the school yet?" That's Jan. Everyone cracks up.

Marla's mom pokes her head in. "Let's go, mamelah! The rabbi says you're giving your speech in five minutes!" When she whisks Marla away, I'm scared I'll have no one to talk to, but right away, Jan comes over.

"You're friends with Vicky, right?"

That again. "Yeah," I say. "Ever since we were little."

"Too bad she got axed from the list. Marla knows how obsessed Vicky is with Aaron Andrews, and she

171

didn't want him paying attention to anyone but her tonight." She shakes her head. "I'll bet V's pretty bummed."

So that's why Marla didn't invite her! It's still hard to believe that I'm here and she's not. I'm not really *happy* about it—I know Vicky feels awful. It's just that every time I think about her lately, I picture us at Katt and Company, where she didn't care one bit whether she was going to get me in trouble.

Tonight I'm on my own. She didn't tell me what to wear. She's not telling me who to talk to or what to say. As terrified as I am, it also feels like a relief.

There's a knock on the bathroom door, and someone calls, "It's starting, ladies!"

A stampede rushes past me. "C'mon," says Jan. "Let's get in there before she starts her speech. Where are you sitting?"

"Oh, shoot! I forgot to check." On the way out, I spot a satin-trimmed table with place cards written out in fancy script. *Miss Melanie Adler—Table 16.*

"Oh, good," says Jan, peering over my shoulder. "You're sitting with all of us."

My heart's about to explode.

The ballroom looks like a pink-and-purple fairyland, with round tables covered in sparkly linens and glowing candles. There are so many different sizes of spoons and forks next to the plates—I hope someone will help me figure out which is the right one to use.

Marla's up front, standing ballerina-straight, gripping a piece of paper. "Thank you, everybody, for coming to my bat mitzvah celebration," she begins. "For those of you who don't know, in synagogue this morning, and every Shabbat morning, we chant the parsha—a portion of the Torah, in Hebrew. Only my family was there for that, so I'm going to talk about my parsha now. It's called Lech L'cha, and it's very special to me because it is about Abraham and Sarah. My Hebrew name is Sarah, in memory of my great-grandmother."

Marla tells us how, in this portion, God gives Abraham all these tests. I'm still so nervous that it's hard to concentrate on anything she's saying. At the next table, Aaron Andrews and Sonny Gellman are fidgeting in their suits. Jerry Finkel's sticking one of his spoons in a water glass and scooping out ice cubes.

Marla's explaining that *Lech L'cha* means "to go out." God's telling Abraham to take Sarah and go away from his home and everything he knows to start something new. "Some people think it also means, 'Go inside yourself, and find the strength to make a change.'"

When she says it, I feel tingly all over. There are so many ways I want to go away from what I know and start something new.

Soon everyone's clapping and shouting "Mazel tov!" and the band starts playing. This guy in a tuxedo who must be the bandleader takes the microphone and calls for all the kids to come out onto the dance floor. He makes us form a big circle, and he calls Marla to the center and tells her to pick a boy to dance with.

"Woo!" everyone hoots when she points to Aaron Andrews, whose ears turn bright red as Jerry pushes him forward. The band plays, Marla rests her hands on his shoulders, and they shuffle back and forth to the music as a photographer's camera flashes at them. Partway into the song, the bandleader calls "Snowball!" and Marla and Aaron each pick someone new to dance with. I can see where this is going. Soon, we're all going to be out there picking partners and stepping out on the dance floor.

The music changes, and instead of playing something slow, the band starts "Smoke on the Water," which blasted on the jukebox every week at the JCC when I used to go to Tweens' Night Out. The floor is packed—even adults are dancing—and when the bandleader says, "Snowball!" one of Marla's cousins, who's about ten years old and a foot shorter than me, comes over and holds his hand out.

"Have fun!" says Jan, cracking up.

Marla's cousin dances like he's holding hot rocks—shaking his hands out in front of him and bouncing up and down on his toes. I have to do something before everyone turns to look at us. I try out the few steps I remember from those Thursday nights at the social hall.

"Hey, I know that dance!" Shari calls to me. "JCC, right?"

I stammer back, "Yeah! Tweens' Night Out!"

She waves me over, and a group of us—the Shimmers and me—do all the steps from beginning to end. We shimmy, wiggle our hips, and dip our shoulders back and forth to the beat. When it's over, Marla says, "That was awesome! Let's do another one!" All those nights of standing against the wall and watching them are paying off, because once Shari starts to move, I know how to do the next one too.

Just as my feet start to burn, the waiters carry out plates of food, the band slows to quiet dinner music, and people head to their tables. I sit down by the swirly number 16 and sip from my glass of water.

"That was fun," says Shari, taking the chair next to me. "And by the way, you're welcome."

"For what?"

"For helping you ditch Marla's cousin. He needs to find someone his own size!"

We both crack up.

It turns out no one else knows which fork to use first, and the waiters bring us different plates of food than what the adults get. Our plates are full of chicken drumsticks and french fries. Within minutes, we've inhaled everything and are back on the dance floor. The Shimmers are smiling at me, and we cheer every time the band plays one of our favorite songs. It's so much fun—everything I dreamed.

The hours glide by, crammed with unforgettable moments. Dance contests. Super-serious speeches by Marla's parents that make people cry. A ceremony where special people in her life come up and light a candle with her. When it's time for me to leave, Marla makes me promise to sit with her and the others at lunch on Monday.

As I feed my coins into the lobby pay phone to call Dad, a part of me wants to stay longer, until the band packs up their instruments and the last guest leaves. But a bigger part of me wants to let my night end now while everything's perfect.

Once I'm in Dad's car, peering back at the twinkling lights of the country club, Marla's speech pops into my head.

Lech L'cha. Go out to a new place. Go inside yourself to a place you've never been.

Maybe tonight I did both.

Chapter 15

"CONGRATULATIONS. YOU'RE A SHIMMER."

The telephone receiver rests between my ear and my shoulder. I wish I could see Dorit's face because even though she says it like a sneer, she sounds sad too.

"It was just Marla's bat mitzvah . . ."

"Well, I'm sure they're thrilled to have one more sheep for their flock."

Dorit makes jabs like this all the time, but today it's more like a punch. "Can we drop the subject? I didn't call to talk to you about the Shimmers."

"Hey, Miss Shimmer, do you mind keeping it down?" Jon says. He combs through the Sunday paper, stuffed with Thanksgiving ads, until he finds the news section.

I untangle the telephone cord and pull it around the corner to the basement stairs. "That's not why I called you," I say to Dorit. "I wanted . . . I'm wondering if everything's okay at home, you know, with your father." I can't believe it was yesterday morning that I left her in her kitchen with her brothers. At the time, I couldn't wait to get out of there, but talking to her now, I know I hurt her. She wouldn't have done it to me.

She doesn't say anything. She's there; I hear her breathing. "Dorit . . . will you talk to me?"

The bubbling of Mom's coffeemaker fills the silence. Dad and I just finished making waffles, and I want to eat them before they get cold. But I know it'll be hard to enjoy them if I don't fix things with Dorit first.

"Please?" I whisper.

Her voice is icy. "How come you didn't tell me you were going until yesterday—were you trying to keep it a secret?"

"No!" I lie. "I just didn't think it was a big deal." It feels like I'm supposed to make a choice right now: Dorit or the Shimmers. I don't understand why I can't be friends with all of them, but it just doesn't seem to be possible.

I pull at a loose thread on my pajama bottoms until it makes the material pucker. "Anyway, tell me what *you* did last night. Didn't those old friends of your parents' come over?"

"Yeah. The Roths." Her voice is flat.

"What're they like?"

"They're visiting the United States from Israel this year. Mr. Roth is a history professor in Boston." She sounds like she's reading their biography.

"So how was it?"

"Well . . ." She takes a deep breath. "At first I thought I'd be bored out of my skull, listening to adults talk all night."

"And then?"

She pauses. "And then I saw him."

My heart takes a jealous leap I don't expect. "Him?"

"Their son, Ari. Fourteen and gorgeous. Curly dark hair and blue eyes." It's strange to hear her talk about a boy—she never has before. There's a distant tone to her voice, like this belongs only to her. "Our parents started telling stories about how we took baths together in Israel when we were babies, so of course we had to get away before we both died of embarrassment. I ended up giving him a walking tour of Ashford."

"In the freezing cold?" I sound like Mom. "In the dark?"

"Yeah," she says. "We took a long walk and talked. *Big deal.*" She says it like she's mimicking me. She wants me to feel bad. "Anyway, our parents grew up together in Israel. Our fathers fought in the same unit during the Six-Day War. They hadn't seen each other in all these years since we moved."

"It must've been cool for them to meet again."

"Why would you think that's cool?" she asks. "They were in a *war* together, not summer camp."

"I just meant . . ."

"Melanie, you've lived in Ashford your whole life. Some things are impossible for you to understand."

It stings, and once again I feel like a little kid around her, one who's all excited about going to a party with the Shimmers instead of caring about serious things like wars.

In the background, Mrs. Shoshani calls her name. "I'd better go. We're moving our last boxes out of storage." When she hangs up, I feel far away from her, like her life is about serious, important things, and I'm young and immature.

The next day at lunchtime, my feet are glued to an invisible hotspot: the table I share with Dorit on my left and the cluster of chairs where the Shimmers sit on my right. I should sit with them. I promised Marla; she wants me there. How bad would it be if I sat there just until Dorit comes?

A squeeze of my shoulder makes me jump. "Ooh!" says Vicky. "Are you finally gonna ditch Dorit? I can't believe it!" Her face lights up like she's watching the boys' basketball team play the last seconds of a tied game.

"I—"

"Take it easy. I'm kidding. Dorit wasn't even in homeroom this morning. What's her deal, anyway? She's always absent."

"She's not here today?"

"Nope." Vicky reaches to grab my shoulder again as I beeline toward the Shimmers' table. "Wait up—if you're going to sit with them, can I tag along?"

It's a strange flip-flop, and I feel a power over her I haven't had since fourth grade when I mastered double Dutch and she was still tripping over jump ropes.

Confidence courses through my veins. "You know they're mad at you, right?"

She chews her lip.

"It's okay," I say, authority growing in my voice. "I know why Marla didn't invite you and why they're leaving you out." I nod to the table where the Shimmers are tossing someone's orange back and forth. "Marla's jealous that Aaron Andrews pays attention to you."

Her eyes grow big. "Really?"

I flip my hair. "Yeah. Everyone talked about it at the bat mitzvah." It's not true; only Jan told me, and I doubt anyone except Marla even cares, but Vicky looks at me like I know everything. A part of me feels mean for acting like I'm better than her, but a whole other part of me wants her to squirm—wants to see what it's like to be the one who belongs.

We drag chairs across the sticky floor. In my two and a half years at Ashford Junior High, I've never seen the lunchroom from this angle.

As soon as I sit down, the clanging of bracelets and smell of bubblegum lip gloss close in on me.

"Melanie!" It's Shari.

Marla follows, digging into a bag of cheese puffs and licking the orange powder off her fingers. "What did you think of my bat mitzvah? Pretty fun, huh?" She shoots a look at Vicky, who suddenly looks super interested in her tuna sandwich.

"It was awesome. I had a blast!"

Jerry Finkel bumps my chair, and I almost fly off. "Hey, Miss Model Student, anything good in your lunch?"

Everyone laughs like he's a funny little puppy who still doesn't know right from wrong, but he's mean. I don't think I could ever get used to being friends with someone who's so mean to everyone except the prettiest girls.

He turns to Marla. "You get busted by The Pits too?"

"Yeah," she says. "The envelope was waiting in our mailbox after my bat mitzvah. At least my mom was still in a good mood from the party, but I'll be stuck at the library this weekend even though it's Thanksgiving break."

"Same," says Jerry.

"We're all going. Shari too."

"What happened?" I ask.

Marla crunches a mouthful of cheese puffs. "The Pits sent out 'unsatisfactory' progress reports to a bunch of us for not turning in any World War I notes. Guess we'll all be at the library this weekend."

I turn to Vicky to joke that she'll have to go to the library if she wants to hang out with the cool kids. But she's focused on something else across the room.

"Whoops," she says, her raspy voice tinged with glee. "Guess I was wrong about Dorit being absent. You're in some deep doo-doo."

I follow her gaze, and there's Dorit at our table, scanning the lunchroom.

Shoot!

If Dorit sees me sitting here, she's going to feel like I'm dumping her for the Shimmers. I know we'll end up fighting.

She sits down and flips the top off a plastic container. Probably the leftover vegetables and rice from our awful sleepover. We never did raid her refrigerator. Or stay up late laughing and telling jokes. Maybe we'll never have that kind of fun together anymore.

I shove a half-eaten sandwich back into my bag. "Sorry, I . . . I gotta go," I tell Marla. "I'll see you later." I don't even give her a chance to say goodbye. Is this how it's going to be now: slinking around so she doesn't catch me with the Shimmers? Will I have to apologize every time I'm with them?

I race around tables, whizzing past the frowning lunch monitor, who points at me to slow down. When I flop into my seat across from Dorit, I'm breathless and sweat's beading around my face.

"You look like you ran across the whole school," says Dorit. "Where were you?"

Not very far, I think to myself, *but miles away.*

Ever since our accident, Thanksgiving has been a mixed bag. Last year, my grandparents flew here, and my cousins even drove in from Ohio. My grandma taught me how to make her stuffing, and now I'm the only person besides her who knows the secret recipe.

This year, we're alone. It's our cousins' turn to host, and with all the snow we've had already, Mom wouldn't travel to Ohio. Not by plane, bus, or train, and definitely not by car.

"Dynamite stuffing, Melanie," says Dad, following Jon and me as we waddle to the sofa to watch *A Charlie Brown Thanksgiving*. "You sure I can't have the recipe?"

"Grandma swore me to secrecy," I tease, "but we may be able to negotiate a bribe."

Mom carries over a pile of crocheted blankets, and we all settle in with our feet propped up on the coffee table. Snoopy's on the screen, wearing a chef's hat and popping up an overflowing kettle of popcorn at the stove. Tonight feels peaceful. I wish home could feel this way all the time.

When the weekend comes, I'm leaning over Dorit's shoulder, munching on a seven-layer bar still left from Thanksgiving, and studying the world map spread out in front of her. We've been holed up in this stuffy library study room for an hour already, since the building opened.

My stomach feels like Mount Vesuvius as I wait for the Shimmers to show up. Usually, the Ashford Library is one of my favorite places on Earth. It's where I showed Mom I could read for the first time. It's where I check out piles of cookbooks and record albums, where I escape deep into books. But today this place is turning me into a jumble of nerves.

"Have you ever noticed how many places have names of fish in them?" I say, dropping coconut flakes on Italy.

Dorit's finger traces a line across the different-colored continents. "Hmm?" She scrawls something about Germany in her notebook.

"Look," I say, flipping to the index. "Sardinia . . . Al*tuna* . . . Whitefish Bay . . . *Minnow*-sota." She doesn't even smile.

"Why are you so antsy? You keep looking out the windows."

"It's Saturday," I say. "I could be watching *American Bandstand* or trying out a new recipe. It's really hard to concentrate."

"We always come on Saturdays," she says. "What's the big deal?"

I want to shout, *THE SHIMMERS ARE COMING!* But I can't. I don't even know how I'll escape this hamster cage to find them. And that's exactly what I feel like in here—caged. Dorit barely looks up from her notebook. I doubt she'll want to take a doughnut break at Gleason's. We haven't even made our usual loop through the library where we each pick out the weirdest and funniest book we can find. In truth, the only thing we've done together lately is divide up the project and plow through it, question by question.

Dorit hands me a massive volume. "Here. Maybe this will help us with some of the definitions."

I flip past pictures of fighter planes and jeeps and scan a timeline of battles before I let the book flop closed. "I'm thirsty—I'm going to get a drink." I can't sit now, not when the Shimmers might already be here.

I swing past the audiovisual station and run my hands over a box of new film strips: *Secrets of the Great Lakes* and *New Frontiers in Space*. When I reach the rows of encyclopedias, I pause and look back. Through the glass window of our study room, I can still see Dorit. She looks so small, papers and books piled around her. Her jaw is set in that way it gets when she's concentrating hard. For a second, I feel like the most selfish person in the world.

I go down to the lobby, which is empty except for a teenage volunteer shelving books in the corner.

An armchair stands nestled against the windows in the bound periodical section. I take two *Time* magazines, "The Push to Impeach" and "Nixon's Jury: The People," both enclosed in plastic binders, and sink into the cushions. I'm starting to understand how important this Watergate scandal is. President Nixon told big lies, and every day there's more and more proof that he tried to cover them up. Jon says we shouldn't trust our leaders anymore. Mom says she's never heard anyone talk that way about a president of the United States.

Jon even does an imitation of President Nixon shaking his head back and forth and holding his hands up in the air, yelling, "I am not a crook!" Everyone at school does it too. Jerry Finkel stuck his head into Girls' Foods before class last week and told a joke: "What did Nixon say when he ruined the soufflé? Answer: I am not a cook!" Mrs. Burnes didn't laugh.

Squeals ring down by the entrance, and my heart jumps. The commotion travels up the stairs. I keep my eyes glued to "Everything You Wanted to Know about Impeachment."

Sit still, Melanie. Play it cool.

"Hiya, Mel!" Vicky singsongs when she reaches me. "Look who I ran into downstairs." Her smile looks desperate as she gestures to Marla and Shari beside her. "I forgot they were coming today!"

Lie.

"Hi, Mel," says Marla as she and Shari start opening the doors to the study rooms, looking for one they like.

Vicky gloms onto me. "Ya gotta help me," she whispers. "They're acting like I'm a leper."

This flip-flop is becoming weirder than ever.

Shari leans out the doorway of a corner room. "Come on in, Mel." My heart leaps as if I'm being invited to go backstage at an Elton John concert.

Vicky looks miserable. I don't know if she'd do the same for me, but it's wrong to leave her out while I go in. "Give me a minute," I tell her. "I'll talk to them."

Inside the study room, Marla and Shari have already scattered chocolate bars and lip gloss tubes across the table. "How do you come here without your parents forcing you?" Shari says. "This room's so stuffy, I think I'm gonna puke."

"So dramatic," Marla says, cracking up. "You always think you're about to puke."

I pull up a chair. "You think I wanted to come here over Thanksgiving break? The Pits got me in trouble with my parents too." It's a big fib, but I'm full of myself because they picked me to join them.

Shari runs her fingers through her perfect *Teen Beat* hair. "*You* got an unsatisfactory progress report?" She doesn't come right out and call me "Miss Model Student," but that's what she means. If I don't play this right, they'll think I'm a prissy, rule-following bore.

"Yeah," I boast. "I'm lucky my parents didn't ground me. You should've seen the letter he sent."

Shari scrunches her face into a skeptical frown. "Wow—a whole letter? I only got a paper with a bunch of check marks in the 'unsatisfactory' column. You must be in *extra* big trouble." She eyes Marla, and they giggle. I try to keep my expression the same so they can't see how stupid I feel.

Shari pushes her denim bag down the table and turns to Marla. "So, what should we do first?" She's not asking which reference books we need or how we should divide up the questions; she wants to have fun. Now I'm scared they'll think I'm not cool enough to be in here.

My heart drums in my chest. "Wait." I summon my courage and slide the door closed. "I have something to tell you." I try not to let my voice shake. I have to show them that I have guts, that I belong in here. "I think you should stop ignoring Vicky. She's sorry if she made you mad, Marla, but she didn't mean anything." I'm all sweaty inside my shirt, and my mouth feels dry. I can't believe I said that.

"Oh, yeah?" says Shari. "Did she make you talk to us?"

"Get real," I say with an edge to my voice. "I just think it's wrong." I'm dying. How am I even doing this?

"Hmm," says Shari.

"What do you think?" Marla asks her. She waits like she won't decide anything unless Shari tells her it's okay. Maybe freezing Vicky out was Shari's idea to begin with.

I don't look down. I want them to know I'm serious.

"Oh, get over it already," Shari finally says to Marla. "You know Aaron likes you!"

Pride floods my chest when they open the door and usher Vicky inside. "Get in here," says Marla.

Vicky enters with a huge smile and curtsies to them like they're royalty. They all crack up.

"You owe Melanie a gigantic thank-you," Marla tells her. "She's an awesome friend."

Hearing her say that should make me feel happy, but instead, a knot forms in my stomach.

Dorit.

I left her sitting alone in our study room almost an hour ago.

"You okay?" Marla asks me. "You're not gonna puke too, are you?"

They want me to stay. And I sure as heck don't want to go back to that social studies jail and watch Dorit draw her World War I timeline poster. Am I being a horrible friend if I stay here?

"Who wants to see this month's *Teen Beat*?" says Vicky. "I have it right here." They gather around the glossy pages, pointing at cute outfits and hairstyles while I stand by the window and chew my lip.

"Ooh, let's do a makeover!" says Marla. "Shari has everything!"

My heart hammers. *Decide, Melanie. Stay or go.*

"Do me!" I yell. It comes out way too loud.

"Cool it," says Vicky, laughing. "Your style does need serious help, but you don't need to get us kicked out of here!"

I try to slow my breathing and calm my heart down before it jumps out of my chest.

I did it. They're going to give me a makeover.

Shari pulls a zippered pouch from her bag and sets it on the table. "Awesome!" she says. "Now sit over here and keep your eyes closed. I want it to be a surprise."

When she brushes the bangs away from my face, I get a nose full of the Spring Meadows perfume on her wrists. It doesn't smell like anti-itch lotion on her. She squeezes something gooey into her palm and works it through my waves.

"Stop scrunching your face and relax," says Marla. "She's not torturing you!"

The two most important Shimmers are giving me a makeover, and I ditched Dorit in our study room. Why wouldn't I be relaxed?

There's the sound of someone rifling through stuff—probably Shari's bag—followed by *plunk, plunk, plunk* on the table.

"Jeez, how much makeup did you bring?" asks Marla.

"Let's start with some blush," says Shari. There's a click of something opening, and a moment later I feel feathery strokes across my cheeks. As a brush glides over my eyelids, I tense up with worry.

"Can I see?" They could be painting a clown face on me, and I'd never know until they finished.

"No peeking," says Shari. "You can use Marla's hand mirror when we're done."

More brushes. A soft sponge dabs my skin.

"Here, Shari; catch this," says Vicky. I recognize the smell of Luscious Lip Treats.

"Strawberry Parfait," says Marla. "Nice."

"I love this mascara," Shari says. A wand strokes the tips of my lashes.

Finally, she pats my face, and a puff of powder tickles my throat. "Okay, everybody—take a look!"

I open my eyes, and Vicky tosses me the mirror. I brace myself in case it turns out to be a joke, but staring back at me is someone with smooth hair, all pulled to one side.

"Wow!" I say. "How did you make me look so good?"

I pucker my lips, pink and glossy, and bat my eyes, deep and dark with mascara. I look like one of them.

"You have to start wearing makeup to school, Mel," says Marla. "You look amazing!"

"Yeah," says Shari, nodding with approval. "I can show you how to do everything I—"

A knock on the door interrupts her.

"Ugh, it's probably the librarian telling us to be quiet."

I open the door and freeze.

"Here you are," says Dorit. "I've been looking all over for you." She tightens her ponytail. My hands fly up to my painted-on Shimmer face.

"Melanie, what's going on?"

I finger my barrette. I need to clear my throat. "Um . . . I guess I lost track of time when I ran into these guys. I didn't plan to leave you for so long."

"Well, it's been over an hour, and we still have a ton of work."

"It's not even due for another week." I feel my snotty voice coming on.

"Why didn't you just tell me you didn't feel like going today? You're not getting anything done hanging out in here."

Vicky jumps in. "She's having *fun*. You know what that is? When people joke and laugh and actually enjoy life."

"Why don't you mind your own business?" says Dorit.

"Oh, it *is* my business." Vicky's on a roll. "I've

been friends with Melanie a lot longer than you have. *Best friends.*"

"Well, Melanie, thanks for ditching me to do all our work on my own. I'm so glad you're having a good time." Dorit's scolding me like I'm a kid who got caught ditching school.

"Can't you lighten up? It's a social studies project, not a report to Congress," I say. Out of the corner of my eye, I see Vicky smile. Shari and Marla watch us in silence, amused looks growing on their faces.

Dorit stiffens. "Why do you think nothing is serious all of a sudden?"

I'm blinking fast. "Just because I don't obsess about the problems of the world every second doesn't make me brainless. Besides, how could I understand such complicated stuff? I've only lived in Ashford for my whole life!"

The Shimmers watch, back and forth, like we're at Wimbledon and it's match point.

"The only thing you care about anymore is being a Shimmer," Dorit snaps. "You must be in heaven hanging out with your idols. Good thing Vicky's here too—she can teach you how to be as big of a phony as she is, someone who only does what you think will make you seem cool."

It feels as if she stuck her foot out and tripped me in the center of the cafeteria, and I'm splayed out on the slippery floor in front of the Shimmers. Everyone watches to see what I'm going to do. I want to run out of the library and disappear forever, but I know if I don't stand up for myself here and now, they'll never think I can be one of them.

"Well, the only thing *you* care about is pretending you're better than everyone else!" My voice rises. "You know all about the world because you've lived everywhere. You already learned everything in your old schools. But you know what? Your life's not perfect. Your dad totally freaked out the other night, when all I did was knock a book off the table on my way to the bathroom! He screamed so loud I'm surprised your neighbors didn't call the police. Stop acting like you've got everything figured out. Stop acting like you're better than me."

For a flash, Dorit looks as if she's about to cry, but in another instant her expression turns cold. "Melanie, you are really going to be sorry you said that." She turns and opens the door to leave. "Oh, and by the way, your makeup looks ridiculous."

Vicky rolls her eyes. "Don't let it hit you on your way out."

Shari sidles up next to me and rests her arm around my shoulder like I belong here with them, and I feel supercharged with energy.

But Dorit turns around, her eyes full of sadness and even pity. "Have fun with your new best friends," she says.

I'm frozen as she shuts the door behind her. I think I've gained and lost everything I've ever wanted all at the same time.

Chapter 16

"MEL-AH-NEEE!"

Inside the gym, the geography fair's going full throttle. The seventh grade holds it every year between Thanksgiving and winter break, when the teachers need something to keep us from dying of boredom. All we eighth graders do is visit the booths.

Marla waves and hollers, "Over here!" Shari and Jan join in too, and a split second later so does Vicky. Maybe I'm imagining it, but ever since the Shimmers froze her out and then took her back, Vicky looks like one of those beauty pageant contestants who tries to stay happy and excited even though they're scared they might get eliminated any second. She's always quizzing me on which Shimmers I talk to on the phone after school, asking if we've made plans without her. I'm used to her being funny and daring, unafraid to say whatever's on her mind, but lately she just agrees with everything they say. It's like she's scared to make them mad again. It must be awful—I feel so lucky they like me.

My Shimmer friends clap their hands up to their cheeks in fake surprise when I reach them at the Kentucky booth. "Did you know the cheeseburger was invented in Louisville?" Marla's reading off some kid's display board.

"And the swimsuit Mark Spitz wore when he won all those Olympic gold medals was made in Kentucky!" Shari points to a tiny pair of swim trunks cut from construction paper.

Jan can barely contain her giggles. "That's it! I'm moving there!"

Kids watch with the same envious look I used to have whenever the Shimmers were near, but now people are watching *me* like that too. Ever since that awful day with Dorit in the library, it's been clear that I'm one of them. It's not like Shari stood up in the cafeteria and announced it, but they've been saving me a seat at lunch every day, and they grab me in the hall whenever they have juicy gossip. Everyone sees it.

Girls from my gym class who never noticed me before perk up when Marla and I reach the Missouri display. "This is *so* cute," one with braces says to me, fingering the bottom of my down vest. It's the same one John Denver's wearing on the cover of his new album, and I love it. I look cool, like I should be out hiking in the Rocky Mountains.

Marla puts her arm around me. "Thanks," she says to them. "I got it last winter when my cousins and I went skiing, but it looks way better on Melanie."

The gym girls smile at me, and I can tell they're taking in the whole scene: me beaming in Marla's borrowed vest, her arm slung over my shoulder, and Shari and Jan blabbing something in my ear about how ice-cream cones were invented in Missouri.

It feels like I'm surrounded by a golden light. I *belong*.

"Oh, look," says Marla, dragging me toward the next table. "Alaska." She plucks a polar bear mask off the display and slips it around her head. "Roarrrrr!" She lunges at me.

"Help! She's after me!" We're cackling as I stumble backward, knocking into a model of a glacier, trying to steady myself, stomping on someone's feet. "Shoot!" I say, turning. "I'm really sorry—"

But time screeches to a stop, and my mouth hangs open like a dog's in a cartoon.

It's Dorit.

She lays such an ice-cold look on me that she might as well be in Alaska. I want to plead with her, *Please don't hate me. I want to be best friends again. I miss you.* But I can't. That's not how it works.

"Oops!" Marla jerks me away. "Looks like we made a wrong turn!"

★ ★ ★

Later in the week, Marla and I are in Girls' Foods, cleaning our kitchen station after making fruit-cocktail muffins. We're wiping down counters, balling up wet rags, and throwing them back and forth at each other, when I blurt out what I've been thinking for days.

"Hanukkah's coming soon. Do you guys want to come over this weekend to make sufganiot?" My armpits sting. *I'm inviting the Shimmers to my house.*

Marla practically spits out her muffin from laughing. "Soof-*what?*"

My cheeks warm. "Soof-gahn-ee-yote. It's Hebrew for jelly doughnuts. That's what people eat in Israel on Hanukkah."

"Oh, did Dorit tell you that?" She says it like she's teasing me.

"No!" I answer fast. I don't want to ever talk about Dorit with the Shimmers again. "I found a recipe in a cookbook I checked out from the library." Immediately, I regret saying it.

"I knew you went to the library for fun," she says, poking my arm. "Stop blushing."

I do go to the library for fun. But admitting it to the Shimmers would be a confession that I'm boring and weird and don't really belong with them.

"So, how about Saturday?" I press, and when Marla says she's in, every uncomfortable feeling floats away.

Saturday afternoon while I'm watching the clock, Mom's at the kitchen table, rubbing cocoa butter into her scars with one hand and writing out our Hanukkah shopping list with the other. "How can it be December already?" She sounds disappointed, like the time passed too quickly, but I'm happy. I can't wait to spend winter break with the Shimmers.

When Marla's mom pulls her car up our driveway and drops off my new friends, I jump out of my chair. They all pile out, but I don't see Vicky. Maybe she's walking over.

"They're here," I tell Mom. I try so hard to sound normal. As they amble up our front walk, knocking hips together, I take a deep breath. "Is . . . is it okay if we hang out by ourselves this afternoon?"

I don't want Mom hovering over us, warning me to watch out for the hot oil or the sharp knives.

Her mouth tightens. "What did *I* do?"

"Nothing!" I say it fast so we won't be arguing when the Shimmers reach our front door. "It's just, I . . . I'm happy my new friends are finally coming over and I want to spend time with them, just us."

"I'll be in the basement, looking for our boxes of Hanukkah candles," she says, pulling the door open. "I'll try not to breathe too loudly."

The Shimmers look different than they do at school. They've got their hair up in high ponytails, and they wear matching sweatpants with stripes down the sides of the legs. They must've planned it.

I take a deep breath and ready myself before I pull the door open. "Come on in!"

Shari charges into our living room. She runs her hands across our wallpaper—green and gold flowers that look like popcorn balls. "Hey, it's fuzzy!" she says. The others rub it too. I never figured that would be the first thing they'd notice. I never figured they'd be inside my house at all.

"What're you looking at?" Marla asks. I expect to see Vicky out the window, bopping around the corner, but there's only a squirrel scampering across the telephone wire.

"Um, did Vicky tell you guys she wasn't coming? I invited her myself."

All eyes turn to Shari, who chuckles. "I may have told her we changed the date," she says, tapping her finger to her forehead. "Whoops!"

Maybe Vicky *should* be worried.

My stomach tightens—it doesn't feel right, leaving her out. Things may not be perfect between us, but I don't want to keep hurting my friends. "I can call her. She only lives a few blocks away. She could be here in a minute."

"No, we're good." Shari's words hang like an exposed wire that everyone's afraid to touch. I don't say anything either. I'm still pinching myself that they're at my house. I can't say anything to make Shari mad.

"What are we standing here for? Where's your bedroom?" says Shari, breaking the silence.

"This way." I point ahead.

They drag me down the hall, examining every embarrassing thing we pass: baby pictures of Jon and me, our brown bathroom with the furry toilet seat cover, and Jon's room with bulletin boards covered in old baseball game ticket stubs and a huge "Wanted" poster of President Nixon.

"Here it is," I say, swinging my door open. "Sorry, it's a mess right now." That's the biggest lie. Ever since they said they'd come, I've been frantically cleaning and redecorating, shoving everything from my craft corner into my closet. Except for my pink shag rug and furry beanbag chair, I changed almost everything. I even made a new macramé piece for my wall, with ceramic beads and feathers.

"Cool aquarium," Marla says, kneeling to gaze at the shimmery fish.

"Oo! Where did you get that?" says Jan, staring at the *Goodbye Yellow Brick Road* album poster hanging next to my closet. "Isn't Elton John the best?"

I don't tell them I had to bake Jon a batch of butterscotch brownies so he'd let me borrow it. And I'm sure not going to let them know that until yesterday, a collage I made of my favorite David Cassidy pictures hung there instead.

Shari reaches for a stack of *Teen Beat* magazines and plops onto my beanbag chair. Marla runs her fingers over a glass cup on my shelf—it looks like an ice-cream sundae, but it's really a candle that smells like strawberries. She takes it in her hands and sniffs. "You have a really cool room," she announces. The others nod with approval.

"Thanks." I feel a squeal rising in back of my throat, but I swallow hard, flip my hair, and give them my best *Teen Beat* smile. "Ready to go to the kitchen? Everything's set up."

"I'll be there in a minute." Shari waves us off, more interested in the "Budget Beach Bikinis" feature she's reading.

"Your house is so quiet," Marla says as we make our way down the hall.

"My dad's running errands," I say. "And my mom's working on a project in the basement." *Because I told her to leave us alone so she wouldn't act weird and scare you away.* "Um, she might be looking through our Hanukkah stuff."

"You mean your presents?" asks Jan.

"No, I mean like our candles and dreidels. They don't go buy us a lot of stuff like people do on Christmas. We each get one big thing." I watch their faces to see if they agree. "This year I want a cassette player."

Marla nods. "My mom does everything all traditional. She says Hanukkah is about spreading light and remembering how we're free to be Jewish in this country. My parents give us coins—gelt—like they got back in Europe when they were little."

I think about the speech Marla's mother gave at her bat mitzvah, saying how their friends are like family, because they have no real family; they all were lost. She promised to carry on Jewish traditions in their memory. I know she was talking about the Holocaust, even though she didn't say it. I had chills.

Shari wanders into the kitchen, her magazine opened to an article: "Self-Confidence—You Can Have It!" She's the last person I'd picture needing that. Wherever she goes, everyone turns to pay attention to her. We're all doing it right now.

"Well, my parents go berserk!" she says. "They give us tons of presents, and my mom throws a big holiday party for her clients. The food is the best, but she doesn't make it—it comes from some fancy caterer. She always says she's the Ready Realtor, not the Galloping Gourmet!" She goes back to *Teen Beat*, and something tells me she's about as interested in cooking as her mother is.

I open my cookbook, with *Property of Ashford Library* stamped on the first page, and flip through until I reach the recipe for sufganiot. Shari's the only person I know besides Dorit whose mom has a job. I see Mrs. Kaye sometimes, dressed up, showing people the vacant house across the street.

"Hey," says Marla, nudging me. "Let's get cooking!" We crack up because it's exactly what Mrs. Burnes says whenever it's a kitchen day. Marla keeps going with her impression. "These soofy-things are going to be *scrumptious* because Melanie and Marla are my star pupils! Oh, and where are my keys? Has anyone seen my keys? I've lost them again!" She's so funny that I'm not thinking about anyone's mother anymore, especially mine stewing in the basement.

"Okay, everyone," I say. "I know this sounds nerdy, but I divided up the recipe so we'll each have something to do." We jump into action around the kitchen table: Marla measuring flour and baking powder, Jan cracking eggs and pouring orange juice into a cup, and me heating oil in a frying pan. Once we've dumped it all together and are taking turns stirring the gloppy mixture, Shari comes in.

"Looks like the stuff I rub on my face at night to get rid of zits." She peers into the bowl before she heads back toward my bedroom, probably to get another magazine.

As Jan adds more flour, the sticky mixture starts turning into dough. We get to work rolling it out and using cookie cutters to make perfect circles. When we drop them into the hot oil, they puff up right away. Soon they're golden brown and I'm fishing them out with a slotted spoon.

"Okay, here's the fun part." After I blow on a doughnut to cool it off, I pick up a metal tube that looks like the thing nurses use to give shots, only this one is lots thicker and there's no needle at the end, just a pointed tip. I scoop little spoonfuls of strawberry jelly into the cylinder and stick this mini-plunger thing into it. When I press it, jelly oozes out of the pointy part.

Jan and Marla gather closer. "Cool!"

"Now, take this chopstick and poke a hole into a doughnut. Then stick this tube thing inside the hole and press. That's how you fill it with jelly. When you're done, you can roll it in sugar."

"Show me how to do it." Marla grabs the jelly squirter from my hand.

Shari rushes back in. "No! *I'm* first." She says it like it's a rule, and Marla doesn't hesitate. She drops the tube into Shari's hand like it's filled with hot oil instead of strawberry jelly.

The first time, Shari pokes too big of a hole with the chopstick and the doughnut falls apart. The next time, it's too small and jelly oozes out all over her fingers.

"I give up," she says, handing it to Marla. "I'm *way* better at makeovers."

Marla and Jan take over, shaping and frying, filling and rolling. The kitchen smells heavenly, and our creations are delicious.

"Yum!" Marla licks her lips after tasting one while it's still hot. She and Jan work over the skillet like they're in a cooking competition.

Shari glances at the clock above our sink. "Aren't you done? This is getting boring."

My heart skips. I hate this worried feeling, like they need to have the best time ever or they won't be friends with me anymore. Sometimes Dorit would come over and all we did was page through the JCPenney catalog or listen to records, and when her mom called and told her it was time to come home, we were both disappointed because even doing nothing together was so much fun.

"I have some cookies you could decorate with icing." I hope she'll start to look interested.

"Yeah, Shari, why don't you ice cookies while we finish?" says Marla, not looking up. "Only a little bit left."

But Shari heaves a breath like she can't wait another second. "That's *it*. You're done. Now it's makeover time!" She pulls the jelly-filled tube from Marla and without warning, she squeezes a bunch of sticky red dots all over my face. I'm frozen because, in a million years, I don't expect her to do that.

"It's a miracle! Her face was a *mess* until I discovered Jelly Magic!" says Shari, fluttering her eyelashes like she's in a TV commercial. "Those ugly scars and lumps just disappeared!"

Everyone's hysterical. I must look so funny to them. But this is not funny to me, especially when I hear footsteps tromp up our basement stairs.

Mom appears in the doorway, holding a box of Hanukkah decorations. I can tell the second they get a good look at her scarred face because their giggling shuts down as fast as a Carpenters' song on Vicky's radio.

"Mom, these are my friends." I wipe the goo off my cheek with the side of my hand. "Marla, Shari, and Jan. You guys, this is my mom."

Something rattles as Mom slides the box onto the table. By the hurt look in her eyes, I know she heard Shari's joke and the laughter. I pray she doesn't think they were making fun of her. I want to say, *How were they supposed to know you have scars all over your face?* But then I wonder, why would anyone joke about that anyway? Dorit wouldn't.

"Have fun," says Mom in a weak voice, her hand running over the zigzagged wounds on her cheeks. She doesn't sample a doughnut or say how good the kitchen smells or ask Marla about her bat mitzvah. When she disappears down the hall, the three Shimmers give one another the eye, like they're going to talk about her the second they leave my house.

Now that I'm alone with them again, I feel more uncomfortable than I ever imagined.

For once, I wish Mom would've stayed.

Chapter 17

THE NEXT DAY AS MR. PITKEWICZ'S CLASS IS about to start, I wait, hoping one of the Shimmers will say they're sorry or ask if Mom's feelings were hurt, but they don't.

"Check out these sufganiot," Shari whispers to the boys, pronouncing it like she's been speaking Hebrew her whole life. "I made them. Aren't they great?" Jerry and Company practically inhale them before The Pits sees, licking every last drop of jelly off their fingers.

Marla and Jan watch with frozen smiles even though we all know Shari was about as interested in cooking as Jerry is in going to a Girl Power rally.

"*We* made them," I whisper to Marla.

"Shh!" she snaps back. It's weird how afraid she is of Shari when they're supposed to be best friends.

Like I'm some expert on how best friends are supposed to act.

While Mr. Pitkewicz is going on about President Nixon's tapes, someone pokes me in the back.

Vicky. I didn't see her come in.

"What the heck?" she whispers. "Shari called and told me we changed it to *next* weekend."

"I didn't know you weren't coming until the others showed up at my house."

"Why didn't you call me? I would've walked over."

"I was going to, but . . . I don't know." I'm too embarrassed to tell her I didn't want to make Shari mad. "I'll make it up to you. Over winter break we'll all do something."

She shakes her head. "I'm going to California for winter break."

When Hanukkah comes the next week, I do get the cassette player I wanted. And an album by Paul McCartney and Wings called *Band on the Run*. Jon gets a new shortwave radio and a book called *The Watergate Follies*, with photos of President Nixon and funny made-up captions.

But over winter break, the days creep by. Marla's family spends every day together, sharing meals with synagogue friends and going on outings to museums and the skating rink. Without her, the other Shimmers don't call me. And Vicky's still so mad that she left for

California without even saying goodbye. One day I go past Dorit's house; their shades are drawn and their lights are off, like maybe they're out of town.

This morning, I'm so bored that I'm watching Jon cut headlines out of old newspapers. His overstuffed album lies open, taking up half of our coffee table.

"Look at this scrapbook," I say. "You are such a Watergate dork!" It comes out meaner than I want it to, but I can't help it—I'm bored out of my skull and in a rotten mood. Fresh glue oozes from the corner of a newspaper headline: *18½ Minute Gap Discovered in Crucial Watergate Tape—Nixon's Secretary Questioned about Possible Erasure.*

Jon yanks the book out of my hands. "Give it back if I'm such a dork. I'm sure you can find something to do with your cool new friends instead of harassing me. What happened to Dorit? At least you acted normal with her." He disappears into the kitchen, the album tucked under his arm.

A wave of sadness rushes over me, hot and full of regret. Every time I think of the horrible things I said to Dorit in the library, I smash the memory down, far and deep, to a place where I pray I can make it disappear forever.

"Jon . . . I'm sorry." A lump that I don't expect rises in my throat. "Come back. I want to ask you something."

He returns with a slice of bread dripping with honey and eyes my trembly lip. "Whoa, don't get so upset. I've been called a lot worse things than a Watergate dork. What's your question?"

I scoot over to make room for him on the sofa and turn to the still-wet page in his scrapbook that shows a picture of a woman in an office. She's twisting and reaching across a desk to answer a telephone, her legs stretched out in front of her. "Who is this?"

Jon licks the honey off his fingers. "Rose Mary Woods, President Nixon's personal secretary."

"This may be a silly question, but what's she doing?"

Jon's face lights up. He'd only be happier if I plunked a hot-fudge sundae in front of him.

"Well, President Nixon finally broke down and turned over some of his secret tapes to the Senate investigators. So, they start listening to one of the tapes where Nixon is talking about the Watergate break-in, and suddenly the recording goes blank for eighteen and a half minutes, like someone erased part of it. It could've proved whether or not he's been lying, but now it's *gone*!"

Jon devours half his slice of bread in one bite. A crumb stays stuck to the corner of his mouth.

"So they bring in his secretary, Rose Mary Woods—that's her in the picture—to testify. She tells them this bogus story that one day she reached to answer the phone and 'accidentally' erased the tape!"

Jon reaches his arms across his body and juts his leg out, like in the picture. He crosses his eyes and sticks his tongue out too. "Accident, huh? Nobody's buying it. They're calling it the Rose Mary Stretch."

I wish I could erase eighteen and a half minutes of *my* life—the minutes when I said those awful things to Dorit. Where's Rose Mary Woods when you need her?

On the last day of winter break, Dad pulls three passes to the Highland Hills Cinema out of his wallet. "Someone in the lab couldn't use them," he says, looking at Mom. "How 'bout it? Jon's at a friend's tonight, and the roads are as clean as our kitchen floor."

Mom doesn't say no.

When dinner's over, Dad grabs the car keys. "Get your coats on. All the popcorn you can eat."

It's his new way of dealing with Mom, ever since the night she freaked out about my sleepover at Dorit's. It's like he decided he's going to push her to do things, even if she's afraid, hoping that'll help. Something tells me it's not going to work.

Minutes later, our car's stuck in standstill traffic. In

the distance, a line of people snakes around the theater. "I knew this was a mistake," Mom says. She's twisting in all directions, trying to keep track of every hazard.

"I should've known," Dad says when we pass the lit-up marquee. "*The Exorcist* is playing. The guy who gave me the tickets said he didn't want to battle crowds tonight. Now I know why."

"We're not seeing that horrible movie!" Fear covers Mom's face.

I've seen news reports about how scary it is—audience members fainting and people running out to the lobby, shaking and crying, afraid to go back in.

"Nope, we're sure not," Dad says. "Any movie where they pass out vomit bags isn't my idea of entertainment. No one's going to feel woozy watching *Lost Horizon*. Plus it'll be nice and empty."

He lets us out near the entrance. A security guard directing traffic waves Mom and me inside while Dad pulls away to search for a parking place. In the lobby, there's a poster of a man standing in silhouette under a streetlight. A note's taped to its stand: *7:30 Show Sold Out*. Crowds jostle us as we inch closer to the ticket counter. Mom's icy hand grabs mine. "Stay with me." Worry drips off of her like sweat off a lifeguard at the Ashford pool.

At the counter, the cashier eyes our passes like we're

handing her counterfeit money. "Hold on," she tells Mom. "Let me get my manager." People in line behind us push into us, grumbling about the sold-out show and scrambling to buy tickets for the one in two hours.

Someone grabs my arm and pulls me out of line.

"Surprise!" says Marla. Shari and Jan are waiting on the other side of the velvet rope. My heart pounds, and for a second I wish they hadn't spotted me. "You didn't tell me you were coming to this!"

"It was kind of last minute. Besides, I hardly talked to you all week."

"Yeah, we were busy," she says, flashing a smile at Shari. I try to read their faces. She told me she was doing stuff with her family.

"Come see *The Exorcist* with us." She squeezes my arm. "My brother's an usher, and he's letting us in."

"I can't. I'm here with—"

"Oh, look!" says Shari. "The boys!"

They drag me across the lobby to the front of the concession line where Jerry and Company are paying for massive buckets of popcorn. "Ooh, Adler," he says in his usual taunting voice. "Are you sure your mommy will let you watch the scary movie?"

"I'm seeing something else." I don't tell him I'm here with my parents or that we're going to some family movie.

"I hope I don't puke," says Shari. "I heard some scenes are really gross."

Marla rolls her eyes. "There you go worrying about puking again. It's gonna be fun—like riding on a crazy roller coaster!" Her eyes twinkle when she says it, like she can't wait to get scared out of her gourd.

Shari wrestles a popcorn tub out of Aaron's arms. "Hey! How about sharing some? You bought enough for the entire theater!"

Marla takes a handful and passes it around. "Here, everyone—help yourselves!"

I'm digging my hand into the buttery kernels when Aaron elbows Jerry. "Whoa," he says. "What's going on over there?"

A security guard whizzes past us toward the crowded ticket line. "Step back, folks, and give us some room." He's barking orders into his megaphone, and my heart flies into my throat.

Mom.

I left her alone.

"Some loser probably thinks they saw the devil," jokes Jerry.

Before the ground can swallow me up, the crowd parts, and the uniformed guard emerges with Mom glommed onto his arm, looking white and gasping for breath. When he clicks the megaphone switch on again, I know he's going to be talking to me.

"Melanie Adler," his tinny voice announces to the scores of people watching, "if you're in the building, meet your mother in the lobby immediately."

The boys double over laughing. I bolt over to Mom, wondering how they can be so mean.

"Mom, I'm here! I'm fine! It's fine!" I try to whisk Mom away from all the people gaping at us, but she won't move.

"I can't breathe. I . . . I'm going to pass out." She's struggling for air, and her voice is loud and full of panic. The crowd circles us and stares. I see one of our neighbors whisper to her husband.

"Call an ambulance!" says the manager. "She might be having a heart attack."

Someone brings a chair, and I ease her into it. "It's okay, Mommy." I keep my voice soft and steady. "I'm right here."

"Where did you go? I . . . I thought . . ." She won't face me. I know she feels horrible that she's making such a scene.

"I'm sorry," I say. Guilt courses through me. I should've known better than to disappear from her in a crowd. "I'd never leave you." I lean my face close to hers, praying she'll stop shaking. "I just ran into my friends. You know, the ones who cooked at our house?

The one whose bat mitzvah I went to?" I want to distract her, but the more I talk, the worse she gets. She starts trembling so hard that she looks like someone threw her into a freezer.

That's when I notice that Marla, Shari, and Jan have followed me. They stand in a row, staring at us like we're the biggest freaks in the world.

"Is your mom *okay*? You were only gone for, like, a minute." Shari doesn't say it like she's concerned. It's more like she's on the verge of laughing. She probably thinks my mom is being overly dramatic. She doesn't understand that Mom's genuinely afraid. Or she doesn't care.

Marla looks as scared as a kitten. She doesn't tell Shari to shut up and mind her own business. She doesn't even meet my eyes. If Dorit were here, she'd put her arm around me and tell me it would be okay. She'd give Shari an earful. And she wouldn't think anything about it was funny.

Shari's circling her finger next to her ear, making one of those "cuckoo" gestures. Mom and I both see it, and there's no way to pretend it's anything other than what it is.

I feel sucker punched, and for a moment I go numb. For the first time, I don't think about how uncomfortable *I* feel or how other kids don't have to deal with this. Instead, I feel horribly sad for my mom. She doesn't want to live like this.

Seconds later, the ambulance arrives and the paramedics lift Mom onto a stretcher. My body throbs with fear, and all I want is for Mom to be okay.

Dad strolls into the lobby as the crowd breaks up. "I had to park across the street," he says. "Did somebody get hurt?" He freezes when he catches sight of Mom lying on a stretcher, a blood pressure cuff wrapped around her arm.

Buttered popcorn churns around in my stomach. "I left her in the crowd, and she got really scared." Tears pool in my eyes. "She couldn't breathe, and she told me she thought she was going to die."

Dad rushes over to the paramedics. He nods when they talk to him, and then he looks like he's explaining something, and *they* nod. My heart is pounding so hard it feels like it's about to crack every bone in my chest. Finally he comes back to me.

"Is she going to be okay?"

"She had a severe panic attack." Dad's nodding as he tells me, like it's exactly what he expected the paramedics to say. "She felt like she was about to die because her body acted like it was in danger, even though it wasn't." He doesn't say it, but I'll bet he knows he shouldn't have pushed her to come tonight.

We follow as the paramedics wheel Mom out to the ambulance. Since they're pretty sure she didn't actually have a heart attack, they don't turn on the siren or the flashing lights, but they still want to check her out in the emergency room. Dad and I follow in our car. The streets are full of potholes now that the ice and snow have melted. Dad and I are silent on the drive, but I know we're thinking the same thing: something has to change.

Chapter 18

THE MONDAY MORNING AFTER WINTER BREAK IS midnight black. I guess when President Nixon declared Emergency Daylight Saving Time to save energy, no one told him that moving our clocks forward in January would mean we'd all be leaving for school in the dark. Mom insists that Jon walk me to the bus stop and wait with me until I've boarded. Before we leave the house, I hug Mom hard, but she still looks full of regret when I wave goodbye.

The bus is quiet, with kids talking in hushed voices as if it's the middle of the night. When I settle into my seat and think about seeing the Shimmers at school, a tug-of-war game plays in my head. When I remember the way they acted at the theater, my heart thumps angry beats. Still, when I think, *The Shimmers won't want to be friends with me anymore because of my weird family,* it really makes me sad. Even though I don't even know if *I* want to be friends with *them* anymore.

But in the lunchroom they call my name and save

me a seat at their table, waving me over like nothing happened.

And I go to them.

I smile and say hi and act as if everything's normal. It's like that time in gym, during a dodgeball game, when a kid whipped the ball at me and it smacked me in the face. No one asked if I was okay, and a lot of people laughed. Even though my nose felt broken, I had to laugh with them. I didn't want the teacher to make me sit against the wall alone, like an injured duckling. I still wanted to be in the game.

Marla pulls me over to the other girls who are jerking their arms up and down and practicing their break-dancing moves. Everyone's obsessed with Michael Jackson's song "Dancing Machine." When Jerry tries doing the Robot in his massive gym shoes, he looks more like a toddler learning to walk. Watching him *is* funny, and pretty soon I'm laughing with Marla and Shari.

See? They're still your friends. They didn't mean anything. Maybe you were being too sensitive.

That's what I tell myself over and over. And I keep saying it as the weeks go by:

As Marla and I make a perfect polka-dot macaroni-and-cheese casserole for our Girls' Foods demonstration.

As we sneak notes to one another while Mr. Pitkewicz drones on about the rise of Communism.

As the Shimmers *still* mess with Vicky—sometimes acting friendly, sometimes ignoring her or whispering in front of her to make her feel left out.

That's when I swallow my feelings the most. That could be me.

One freezing afternoon in February, I'm crossing the park and see Vicky sitting on a swing. Ever since Hanukkah when the Shimmers came over without her, she's found reasons not to walk home with me. At least I'm not stuck waiting for her by my locker every day, but it still feels weird.

"Hi," I say. "You waiting for someone?"

She rubs her mittened hands together, and when she talks, little clouds puff around her mouth. "Yeah. Jan's coming over. She told me to meet her here while she runs to turn in her permission slip for that field trip next week." She's squinting behind me toward the school with a look of hope and worry swirled together.

Before I left, I saw Jan follow Shari out to the buses, and she didn't look like she was coming back.

"What's the problem?" Vicky pulls her scarf tighter.

"Nothing. Just . . . it's awfully cold to wait out here." I pause, knowing she won't like what I say next.

"And I saw Jan, and she was getting on the bus. I don't think she's—"

"She'll be right here," snaps Vicky. "You don't know everything."

I slide onto the swing next to her. "Vicky, they're playing with you again." The chain squeaks as I drift back and forth. "Why do you want to be friends with them when they're so mean to you?"

"*Me?*" She pulls her swing backward and stops on tiptoes. "What about you? I heard about what happened at the movie theater. They made fun of your mom in front of everyone, and look at how buddy-buddy you still are."

My neck burns. She said out loud what I've been thinking for weeks. "*You* joked about her too," I fire back. "Or don't you remember all the times you called her a worrywart?"

"It's not the same, and you know it. I tried to get you to lighten up, not embarrass you."

Because teasing someone about the thing they're most worried about in the whole world, the thing that gives them nightmares and fills them with dread, is a great way of helping them deal with it.

"You don't understand," I say. "Maybe it's not even your fault. Maybe you can't." As soon as the words leave my mouth, I realize that's exactly what Dorit kept saying to me every time I pushed her to tell me what was wrong. Regret vibrates through my body. I was so sure I knew what Dorit needed. I should've listened to her.

"I want to be a Shimmer," Vicky says, as certain as if she were reciting her name and address. "Maybe it won't be easy, but I'm not starting high school next year as a nobody."

High school? I try to imagine next year, always worrying about whether the Shimmers like me or not. Letting them say any mean thing that crosses their minds and swallowing my anger and hurt so I don't make waves. Tiptoeing around like Marla, who won't even sneeze unless Shari says it's okay.

As I jump off my swing, a voice calls from the street. "Hey, Vicky! Thanks for waiting!"

Jan.

Vicky pops up and waves wildly. She shoots me a smug look, as if I don't know what I'm talking about. But she's wrong—I know a lot. I know I can't be friends with people who make me afraid to say how I'm really feeling. Or who think all Mom needs is to relax a little. Disappointment settles in my stomach like a bucket of cement.

Being a Shimmer is never going to make everything in my life perfect.

Chapter 19

MY HAIR IS SOAKED BEFORE WE EVEN GET ON the school bus. This "winter discovery" field trip is going to be miserable. For the past week we've been preparing for it by watching the most boring film strips about animal hibernation and winter behavior, even though we've been dragged on this same trip every year since fifth grade. Three years in a row of trudging through the woods, studying animal poop, and standing around while the nature guide tries to tap a maple tree for syrup.

"Eighth graders, take your seats! We're scheduled to depart in three minutes." Miss Roole checks her thick, military-issued watch. Everyone groans, but she doesn't cave in. "It's the end of February, people. That's why the permission slip said 'rain or shine.'"

"Man, I faked every sickness I could think of, but my parents still made me come," Jerry says, lumbering up the bus steps behind me. "How much you wanna bet The Ruler's gonna make us march in the rain?"

Marla catches my eye from the seat she's sharing with Shari and wags her finger up and down at the getup Miss Roole's wearing. It *is* ridiculous: green army pants, lace-up boots, and a rain poncho that could cover the entire eighth grade. She even has a pair of binoculars looped around her neck. It looks more like she's ready to chase Communists than visit a nature center, but I only give Marla a half-smile. I don't know how to act anymore. The Shimmers aren't my real friends; I gave up my real friend to become one of them.

And Vicky's so thankful the Shimmers are being nice to her that she pays about as much attention to me as she does to the drone of Miss Roole's safety announcements. When Jan scoots over and makes room for her to sit down, she's in heaven.

"Move it, Adler," says Jerry. "You're not picking your seat for a Zeppelin concert." The boys hoot like he said something hilarious. Most of the rows are already filled, and I don't know where to go. I have no idea where I even belong.

"Stay put, Miss Adler," says Miss Roole, checking the sheet on her clipboard. "You're sitting with me."

I wish she were joking.

The bus doors creak shut, and the engine growls. I can't stop shivering. Good thing I grabbed an old pair of Jon's galoshes and his lined raincoat on the way out of the house. I can imagine Dorit saying how ridiculous it is to freeze just because you want to look cute.

Where *is* she, anyway? She's not up here by the driver, and she's definitely not in the center with the Shimmers. Maybe way in the back?

"You can stop looking for Dorit," Vicky says to me. "She's not here today. I saw her name on the 'Absent' list when I turned in my permission slip."

Shari unwraps her bubble gum when Miss Roole isn't watching. "She's the one from the library, right? You two had that big blowup?" She stuffs the fruity wad in her mouth and starts chomping.

My face heats with shame. "Yeah. Dorit Shoshani. She *was* my friend."

Shari leans forward in her seat to take in my expression. "Wait—are you telling me that you didn't hear?" she says to me.

"Hear what?"

She glances at the others. "Should we tell her? She's the only person on Earth who doesn't know."

Giggles.

"What is it? Just tell me!" I hate how desperate my voice sounds.

Shari shakes her hair. "Would you cool it? It's not

that big of a deal. My mom's selling their house. Dorit's moving back to Israel at the end of the school year." Shari says it like she's known about it forever.

The bus swerves around a corner, and I hold on so I don't lose my balance.

The sky is even darker by the time our bus pulls back into the school parking lot, and fat snowflakes are starting to fall. Instead of walking straight home, I squish along in my wet shoes, down the hill to Dorit's block. All day, while we slogged through the dripping woods, it was the only thing I could think about. I have to go past her house to see for myself—I wouldn't be surprised if Shari made it up to see me squirm.

On Dorit's street, trees stand bare. I steel myself, as if a nurse is coming at me with a long needle.

FOR SALE
PREMIER REALTY
SANDY KAYE—THE READY REALTOR!

A sign sits mounted on her front lawn, and I can't pretend it isn't there.

I jog back toward my house, huffing up a hill, pain

slicing my side. It's late. Mom might've already sent Jon out to look for me.

I hear the hum of a car slowing behind me, and I swallow hard. Maybe Mom's right; maybe I shouldn't be walking alone.

"Hey!" a voice calls out the open window. I turn. It's Dad! He's never home from work this early. And *Mom's* in the passenger seat, dressed up like she came from a meeting.

"What are you doing here?" I say.

"We'll meet you at home in a minute. And we picked up pizza for dinner."

It's weird. Mom didn't look worried or scared, even with the snow falling. They didn't even ask me why I'm late.

Minutes later, they call Jon and me into the kitchen to eat early. I rest my hands on the cardboard pizza box, still warm, as they unpack containers of minestrone and plastic spoons.

"We have something to tell you," Dad says.

When Mom sees my face crumple, she jumps out of her seat and wraps her arms around me. I struggle to blink back tears; I can't handle any more news today. "No, honey," she says. "It's *good*. Don't worry."

Hearing Mom, of all people, say "don't worry" sounds so strange and funny that I'm laughing and crying at the same time. "What's going on?"

"I signed up for a new program that helps people who've had a trauma. A psychologist is doing a study, and she thinks people who've had something really scary happen to them have a lot in common, even if the scary things were all different."

Scary things. Like waking up in a hospital and not knowing if your family is still alive. Or fighting in a war and having a bomb explode near your friend.

Mom passes out paper plates and napkins. "I had an interview today at the hospital, and I qualify for treatment. I'll be meeting with Dr. Crosby twice a week, once by myself and once as part of a group with other people like me."

This is the calmest I've seen Mom in ages. It's like she's finally facing the thing she's feared most.

"I know how hard things have been, sweetie," she says, watching me rub my eyes. "I see how you hurry home from school every day so I won't panic. And how my worrying upsets you."

Wow. She's never admitted it before. I bury my face in her chest.

Mom strokes my hair. "I'm scared. But I'm going to be brave."

My throat feels so choked that I can't speak. I let go of everything and cry.

Later, Dad and I watch the evening news—him in his easy chair and me flopped down on the sofa. The television screen shows a film clip of tanks, then a map of Israel and Syria. I sit up.

"Three Israeli soldiers have been killed in the past two days of clashes between the countries," says the reporter. "Although the war officially ended months ago, fighting rages on."

"You okay?" Dad asks.

"The fighting in Israel . . . I thought the war was over."

He rubs his forehead. "Seems like that war will *never* be over." I don't ask him what he means.

★ ★ ★

Jon shows me a newspaper article about how a passenger discovered a bomb on a bus in Tel Aviv right before it was about to explode. That night, I dream that Dorit and I are riding the bus to the mall when someone yells at us to jump off because it's about to blow up. I wake up with tears in my eyes.

The next day, when I see Dorit across the cafeteria, sitting with the neighborhood kids, I want to tell her about the dream. But I can't. Maybe I'll never be able to tell anyone.

I wake up shivering before my alarm goes off. Mom's opening windows, letting the fresh air blow in, like it's already spring.

Something's changing about her already. It's tiny, barely noticeable, but it's like she's made up her mind to do something different. To be brave even though she's scared.

Spring is supposed to mean hope, and new beginnings, and all that stuff. If Mom can do it, I can too.

Chapter 20

"WHY ARE YOU SITTING OVER HERE WITH THE cooking class weirdos?" Marla whispers at lunch.

"I thought I'd try something new," I say. "Turns out they're really nice. We're talking about signing up for the Junior Chefs summer program at the high school."

Marla wrinkles her nose. "Whatever. Come on— Shari has a new audience."

Across the room, Shari's surrounded by those girls from gym who only started talking to me once I became a Shimmer. I can tell by the way they're standing that they haven't been invited to sit down, but when Shari passes her new scarf around and lets everyone try it on, I think they're going to need smelling salts to be revived.

I want to tell them, "Don't get sucked in. They're not as great as they seem." But they'd never listen. *I* didn't when Dorit said it to me. Disappointment weighs me down like the lead vest I had to wear when I got x-rayed after our car accident.

When I don't jump up to follow Marla, she warns me, "You better be careful or someone's going to take your spot." I don't know if she means my seat at the lunch table or my place in their group, but either way, I don't care.

"Come sit over here with me," I say. It's a pointless test; she'll always pick the Shimmers over me.

"Nooo, that's okay." She chuckles, holding her hands out in front of her and backing away like she's avoiding something toxic.

That's when Mom's voice rings in my head. *I'm scared, but I'm going to be brave.* It propels me out of my seat after weeks of trying to forget the way the Shimmers laughed at her. After weeks of telling myself they didn't really mean the awful things they said. After weeks of trying to convince myself that being a Shimmer is more important than *anything*.

Mom's words make my heart drum with enough anger to push me forward. Pretty soon I'm shoving chairs out of the way and squeezing between tables until I reach Marla.

"I knew you'd change your mind," she says. She stops next to the condiment station where I avoid a blob of ketchup smudged on the corner.

"I didn't change my mind—I'm not moving over there."

"Suit yourself."

"You're awfully sure of yourself when it's just the two of us," I say. "Too bad you can't be like that when it really matters. Like at the movie theater."

Marla's face goes as blank as if I asked her to demonstrate the five uses of a paring knife. "I totally have no idea what you're talking about."

"You don't remember what everyone said about my mom when she couldn't find me? They laughed and called her crazy, and you stood there and watched."

Now her cheeks look pale.

"I know I'm not best friends with Shari and Jan like you are, but I thought at least they'd wonder if my mom was okay instead of making fun of her. And I thought you *were* my friend. Even if you don't know all about my mom, you didn't have to stand by while they said those mean things. How could you do that?"

Marla's eyes brim with tears. "I don't know," she finally says.

"I do." I jut my chin in the direction of the Shimmers' table. Shari clears her throat at us in this exaggerated way like she's fed up with waiting. No one ever makes *her* wait. "Look at how Shari's watching us. Her eyes are all bugged out because she wants you to come back and you're still talking to me. Well, go ahead. You're so scared of losing your place in the Shimmers that you can't even say what you're thinking unless you know she'll agree with you."

Marla heaves a shaky breath. Right when I think she's about to say she's sorry, her eyes dart over to Shari, and she stays silent.

There was a time when I never could've imagined saying these things to her, or to any of the Shimmers. Now I can't imagine holding it all inside.

"I can't sit with any of you ever again. I can't be friends with you." When I walk away from Marla and back to the kids from cooking class, for the first time ever, I don't care who's sitting at the center table.

A few days later in social studies, the lights are off and Mr. Pitkewicz isn't here yet. Everyone's gathered around Jerry and his new watch. It's called "digital" because instead of a round face with hands that show the time, it's square, with numbers that light up. He's such a show-off, pressing buttons to see how long Aaron Andrews can hold his breath and to tell us what time it is in Japan.

When I see Dorit sitting alone at her desk, my pulse speeds out of control. I've been too scared to call her, and I've started dozens of apology letters, but I end up throwing them away. They seem so weak, nothing like what

I really mean. I know this is a horrible moment to try, right before The Pits marches in, but I can't help myself. Even if she won't forgive me, at least it'll be a start.

"Dorit, can I talk to you?" I breathe like I ran three laps around the track.

When she finally looks up and her eyes meet mine, I feel about as important as the bug smushed on the window. I'm readying myself to say I'm sorry, but she stops me cold.

"Not now, Melanie."

My whole body feels the blow.

Seconds later, Mr. Pitkewicz bursts in looking flustered. "I need someone to run down to the office ASAP and see if my grade book's there." He's tearing through his briefcase, pulling folders out and scattering them on his desk.

"I'll go!" I don't think when I yell it. I just want to leave.

The Shimmers laugh. Someone murmurs "Miss Model Student" as I race through the doorway, but I don't even care. They don't know anything about me.

Down the hall, Vicky's at her locker. She's still wearing her jacket and carrying her book bag like she just arrived.

"Whoa," she says when she sees me. "Who punched you in the gut?"

"No one. It's . . . I'm going to the office for The Pits. He thinks he left his grade book there."

"I'll go with you. The secretary said she made up a whole pad of late passes with my name filled in already!" She squeezes my arm. "Hey, are you okay?"

"No." My voice catches.

"You wanna spill?" She's not rolling her eyes or making rude remarks or trying to impress anybody. It's just the two of us.

And it's weird, but before I can answer, we're wrapped in a hug that lasts a long time.

"You're snotting on my shirt," Vicky teases.

When I try to laugh, it comes out more like a gasp for air.

"What's going on?" Her face is so close I can smell her bubblegum Luscious Lip Treats, reminding me of our shoplifting fight a few months back. I didn't think I could feel any sadder about the state of my friendships, but that sinks me even deeper.

"I . . . I've been thinking a lot," I say, my voice trembly, "about how everything is changing, like all at once. Dorit's moving across the ocean, and I'll probably never see her again. And the Shimmers—I'm done with them. You can have them. I did so many mean things, even to you, just so they'd like me, and it turns out that *I* don't even like *them*."

I shake the hair off my face like I'm trying to straighten out the mixed-up ideas I've been holding in my head. Everything I thought I knew about friendship turned out to be as unreliable as the sun on Shimmer Pond.

Vicky, the friend I've known since I wore size 2 sneakers, holds my arm as I continue: "It makes me wonder about you and me. Like, next year, in high school, are we even going to be friends? When we see each other in the hall, are we going to just wave and keep walking?"

She wasn't expecting me to ask this, I can tell. Her eyes glisten in a way I hardly ever see, and for once, her raspy voice stays quiet. "We'll always be friends," she finally answers. "I mean, I've known you practically as long as I've known my *family*." Her voice strains, trying to convince us both.

"Yeah. My mom always called you 'the extra Adler' when we were little." A flood of memories rushes at me: learning to roller skate in front of my house, building snowmen and dressing them in Dad's hat and sweater, and sometimes, doing absolutely nothing except snacking on soda and chips while playing Go Fish.

"But we're older now, and we're going in such different directions. And . . . I think that's okay." I feel calm, like a load has lifted from my chest. "You'll always be the first best friend I ever had—that will never change."

Vicky bites her lip and blinks back tears, looking at me like I'm someone she's never seen before. Maybe I am.

When we reach the office, I stop. Dorit's mom stands at the counter holding a packet of forms. She smiles at me the same way as always, like no time has passed, like maybe she doesn't know what happened between Dorit and me. I barely remember to wave when Vicky grabs her late pass and leaves.

"So many papers to sign, just to take away some files," she says.

I nod at her because I know she must be getting Dorit's records to bring to her new school in Israel. "Does it take that long?"

Mrs. Shoshani lowers her glasses.

"For the school to give you her records, I mean. It's only March now."

She shakes her head. "We leave next week, Melanie, when spring break comes. We will be home in time for Pesach." She uses the Hebrew word for Passover.

My heart plummets. Shari said they weren't leaving until the end of the school year.

I have one week to make things right between me and Dorit. Because after that, she'll be gone.

When Dorit sees me heading toward her at lunch, she whispers something to Lisa and Charlene. "Why don't you leave her alone already?" Lisa says as they whisk her out of the cafeteria.

And for the next three nights in a row when I call her house after dinner, it doesn't matter if it's her little brothers or her parents who answer—all they say is, "She can't come to the phone."

It's the last hour of the last day Dorit will ever be in school with me, and I'm trapped way up in the bleachers while a theater troupe performs scenes from *Hamlet* under the basketball hoop. Tears of regret and shame prick the backs of my eyes, blurring my vision as I search for her.

"Adler, why do you always have that end-of-the-world look on your face? Don't tell me you're sad there's no school for a whole week." Jerry sticks his lower lip out and screws up his face like he's about to cry. I wish he'd shut up and let me concentrate on finding Dorit in this crowded gym.

If I don't see her now, I may never see her again.

Miss Roole blows the whistle around her neck. "Let's give a big thank-you to the Bard Bunch for a fine performance this afternoon!" Students clap, though they're probably just excited that the school day's about to end. The lump that's been growing in my throat all day is as thick as the crowd around me. Where is she?

The bell rings, and cheers fill the gym.

"Ladies and gentlemen, you're free to go," Miss Roole booms into the microphone.

I'm blinking fast as I plow through groups of kids, scouring the crowd for a girl with a toffee-colored ponytail. Everyone's pouring out of the gym with jackets and book bags, and I'm spinning around, looking everywhere. I grab Charlene and Lisa and ask if they've seen Dorit, but they shake their heads and run together to catch the bus. I dart outside, but all I see are kids climbing into school buses and the Shimmers whooping it up by the flagpole.

Where is she?

I'm about to run back and search the gym again when a horn beeps behind me. Mrs. Shoshani calls out from the open window of their station wagon. "Have you seen Dorit? I have a babysitter for only a short time."

"I'm here, Ema," Dorit calls from the school doorway. She's walking beside Mr. Pitkewicz, chatting away. I can't accept that she'll say goodbye to him and not me.

I'm scared, but I'm going to be brave. I say it to myself like I believe it.

When Dorit steps away from The Pits, I wave, but she looks past me.

"Dorit! Can I talk to you?" I'm yelling. I'm out of breath. "Please!"

"*What?*" There's a bitter tone to her voice that she never used when we were friends.

"I just wanted to say—"

"Can't you see my mother is waiting?"

The words I want to say vaporize like steam from a kettle. I stand frozen as Dorit gets into her car, and Mrs. Shoshani drives away.

Every day of spring break, I call her house. I try in the morning, and I try after dinner, right at the time when we used to talk every night. Someone always takes my message. No matter who in her family answers, I say, "Please tell Dorit that I'm so sorry and I really need her to call me back." But she never does call back. Each time I hang up, dread rushes over me. I'm terrified that the next time I call, her phone will be disconnected and they'll be gone.

At the end of the week, I let her phone ring for a

full ten minutes, but this time no one answers. Am I too late? I picture her climbing into an airport shuttle with her family, waving goodbye to their house as they pull away, leaving it behind, dark and empty.

In seconds, I yank on my sneakers. I rush outside to the garage and snag my bike.

"Hold on! Where are you going?" Mom's close behind.

"To Dorit's," I say, scrambling onto my seat. "I'll explain later." I can't believe it when she nods and lets me go without another word.

I pedal like I'm in the last lap of an Olympic race. I've thought of a million things I could say to make Dorit understand how sorry I am and how much she means to me, but I know that the best words in the world might not be enough.

I'm gasping for air, sweat drenching my shirt, when her house comes into view. The sight of her brothers sitting on the front step, thumbing through a stack of baseball cards, fills me with relief.

"Mellie!"

The second I hop off my bike, I become a human jungle gym.

"We missed you! How come you never come over anymore?" Benny swings from my arm.

"We're going on an airplane after Shabbat. We're

moving to Israel." Natan's face looks serious as he winds a rubber band around his wad of cards.

I press my nails deep into my fist to keep from crying. "I know. I'm going to miss you. Is Dorit home?"

"No!" says Benny.

"Yes, she is," says Natan, giving him a look. "Stop lying."

"But didn't she say we should—"

"Never mind him," says Natan.

Her brothers lead me inside, but the house doesn't look the same as it did last time I was here, the night of our awful sleepover. Dorit's father chatters on the phone in Hebrew with a lilt in his voice, like he's excited. Their furniture is gone. Labeled boxes are stacked against the wall in rows so perfect that it's obvious the Shoshanis have done this a bazillion times. A hollow feeling grows in my middle.

"Dorit!" Her mom sends me a sympathetic look, giving me a drop of courage.

A voice from the hall startles me. "What're you doing here?" Dorit glares at me as she steps over a giant garbage bag.

My tongue is practically stuck to the roof of my dry mouth. "I want to apologize . . . and to say goodbye."

Dorit's mother shoos the boys outside to play and disappears into the kitchen with her father. The two of us are finally alone together. My heart pounds; this is my chance.

"That day at the library, when I said those awful things to you, and *about* you, in front of everybody— I'm so sorry. I know how much I hurt you." I swallow back tears. "Wanting to be a Shimmer is no excuse for how I acted. For so long, I just wanted to be included, to be one of them. To belong. But they've never been my true friends. *You* were a true friend, and I ruined everything." I take a shaky breath. "I threw away our friendship, and I'm sorry."

Instead of responding, Dorit stares at the garbage bag. I wait, praying for her to answer.

Finally, she exhales. "Okay. Well, thanks for stopping by." She walks me to the front door.

That's it?

"Dorit, I want to make things right before you leave."

"Why? So you can feel better?"

"I don't think I'll ever feel better for what I did to you." I wipe my eyes. "But we were best friends. We understood each other, and we meant so much to each other. Right? I just—I don't want things to end like this."

More silence.

"Would you at least take a walk with me? You don't even have to talk. I just want to spend some more time with you before you leave."

For once, she doesn't look away, like maybe she's actually considering it. But a moment later, she opens her front door and says, "Bye, Melanie," in a formal voice. I want to keep trying—to remind her of all the special times we had together. But I can feel that it's too late. She ushers me out and slams the door behind me.

As I stumble to my bike, Dorit's brothers are all over me. "Don't go!" they say. "Stay and play ball." Mrs. Shoshani comes outside. Her sad eyes let me know she heard everything.

"She is tough like her abba," she says. "That's good when you are surrounded by enemies, but around friends . . ." She shakes her head.

I spot Dorit looking out the living room window. I can't tell if her expression shows regret or relief that I'm leaving. "I'm going to ride around the neighborhood," I say more to myself than to Mrs. Shoshani. "In case she changes her mind."

Pedaling away, I clutch my handlebars and pick up speed. I ride through the park, bouncing over gravel and wood chips, finally slowing down when I reach our school.

Ashford Junior High. I think back to that first day in Miss Roole's office when Dorit sat in that flimsy chair, holding the school handbook. Even though we'd just met, something about her seemed so familiar.

I had a hunch that she hated her freckles as much as I hated mine.

Turning away from school, I pedal straight uphill. My bike wobbles as I reach the top and cross the street to the pool—the first place we went together last summer. It's closed, of course, but I stand at the fence, peering in, remembering our races and cannonballs, and the feeling of the warm pavement on our towels as we listened to the Carpenters on my radio. That was when I knew Dorit was becoming my best friend.

I ride past the tennis courts where we pretended to be Billie Jean King at Wimbledon. It starts to drizzle, matching my gloomy mood. Do the good times we had here count anymore? Or did I wash every good memory away?

Raindrops mix with my tears as I ride past my house. I let them run down my face as I pedal without stopping. It hurts to remember the sleepovers, the dances we made up, and the songs we sang together. But what hurts most is remembering the night we discovered all the scary things we had in common with our families and the way it felt to finally have a friend who understood.

As I'm about to cross Ashford Avenue for The Scoop, a horn honks behind me. I pull over and squint to make sure I'm seeing correctly.

Dorit climbs out of the station wagon and stands on the curb. Her mother waves and pulls away.

My voice shakes. "W-what are you doing here? How did you find me?"

"My ema said you were going to ride around. Since this was one of our favorite spots, I thought you might come here." She pauses. "It's not right for me to leave without talking to you."

I break our awkward silence by asking, "Can I buy you a scoop?" She shakes her head and sits on the bench in front of Buck's Hardware. I kick at a pile of helicopters—that's what I called the maple seeds when I was little. But I'm not little anymore. I face Dorit, afraid to say anything after the way she shot down my apology. Finally I ask, "How's your father doing?"

Dorit sighs, and something in her opens the tiniest bit. "Better. Once my parents decided we were moving back to Israel, things weren't as bad. He said he finally realized he can't run away anymore. He needs to be back where he belongs, where *we* belong. He said we're Israelis, and Israel is our home."

"I really thought you were staying here for good."

"So did I. We never bought a house any other place we've lived. My parents tried so hard to make this our home. The night you slept over—when my father screamed—I think that was it for them. They knew he'd never really settle in here. And after the Roths came to visit, my parents couldn't stop talking about moving back."

Understanding, I nod.

Cars whiz down Ashford Avenue. "How's your mom?" she asks.

"She's better too," I say. "She's in a new counseling program called 'Survivors of Trauma.' Everyone in her group went through something really scary and hard. There are even people who fought in Vietnam. And they all have things in common. Bad things, I mean, like nightmares and memories and fears about safety."

"*We* could've told them that," says Dorit.

I nod. It's so true.

Music spills out from The Scoop. My throat is suddenly one big lump. "Dorit?"

For the first time in so long, she looks at me like she cares.

"I can't force you to forgive me." A single tear tracks onto my T-shirt. "I understand if you hate me."

Dorit tightens her ponytail. "I don't hate you," she says. "I don't know exactly *how* I feel. But I don't think we'll ever be the same kind of friends again."

It doesn't feel like a punch when she says it, more like someone yanking off a bandage on something that's been hurting for a long time. Dad would say I've "learned something the hard way."

"I'm still glad you're here now," I say. "I'm really glad we talked."

She nods. "Me too."

After I buck Dorit back to her house, I can't pretend to be strong, not even in front of her little brothers. I sob.

"Come visit us in Israel," Mrs. Shoshani says as she hugs me goodbye.

Mrs. Shoshani pulls Dorit in, and her brothers latch onto my legs. When we finally pull apart, I reach into my pocket and take out a macramé key chain I made. I hand it to Dorit.

"It's beautiful," she says.

"For your new house. And maybe someday, I'll get to see it?"

"Maybe," she says. "Someday."

I tuck that hope away in a special place in my heart.

Epilogue

IT'S AUGUST. THE EIGHTH, TO BE EXACT.

Everyone says we'll never forget where we were or what we were doing on this day.

Jon's been planted in front of the TV since dawn, and even the hamburgers and grilled onions Dad and I made together haven't budged him from his spot on the sofa. President Nixon is scheduled to speak at eight o'clock.

I'm holding the letter that came from Dorit today, finally, after all these months. I keep reading it over and over, as if it'll bring her closer. The tissue-thin envelope is postmarked June 30, more than a month ago. My reply will be ancient history by the time she gets it.

"What did she say?" Mom asks. I squint at the almost-transparent paper, with *Hebrew University of Jerusalem* printed on top. It's where her father is a professor now. Like her math homework, her words are tiny and written in neat rows.

I run my finger along the letter. "First, she explained why it took so long to send me a letter. She said she had so much to tell me that she kept writing and writing. Then she described getting off the plane—how the first thing she noticed was soldiers with machine guns all over the airport, but then she realized they're everywhere."

Mom frowns. Luckily, the rest of Dorit's letter is full of happier details.

"And she finally saw her grandparents for the first time since she was little. She went through the old things they'd been storing for her family all these years—her old toys and baby clothes. Then her parents went to buy a new car while some family friends took her on a tour of Jerusalem."

I close my eyes and imagine Jerusalem based on the posters at the JCC. I wonder if she went to the Western Wall.

"Sounds like she's home," says Dad. I wish it weren't true, but it is.

I lick a row of stamps and plaster them on an overseas envelope. "I already wrote back. I told her about being in the Junior Chefs program at the high school this summer and the kids I met who love cooking as much as I do. Oh, and about how I'm learning to knit now."

I think back to the recipes I've made with the Junior Chefs: fudge, popcorn balls, homemade ice cream. And I think of how my new friends and I rode our bikes to The Scoop and even went to the Ashford pool after class. It feels like a big relief to spend time with kids who seem like me. We may never be as close as Dorit and I were, but I think we'll stay friends once high school starts. We're already talking about sitting together at lunch.

"I told her about high school orientation in that gigantic building too," I say. "And the new family who bought the house across the street. And I told her about President Nixon speaking tonight, but she'll know about it by the time she gets this letter." I slip in next to Mom and Dad on the sofa while Jon shushes everyone and turns up the volume.

President Nixon sits behind a desk, holding a wad of paper and looking defeated. He explains that he's never been a quitter but that America needs a full-time president. Continuing to fight to prove his innocence, he says, will take time away from the important issues facing the country. "I shall resign the presidency effective at noon tomorrow."

Jon's fist shoots up in the air. "Yes!" He looks like a football fan cheering a touchdown, only I know Watergate's not a game to anybody.

I know Mom and Dad are relieved that Nixon's resigning, but they don't cheer like Jon. They just look sad—even disappointed. "They sure don't make presidents like they used to," Dad says. Maybe Mom and Dad have realized, like I have, that people aren't always who you expect them to be.

The speech only lasts for five minutes, and right afterward a panel of newsmen starts rehashing every word. A picture of Gerald Ford flashes on the screen. He's being sworn in as president tomorrow.

I lick the seal on my letter, and without anyone freaking out about where I'm going, I jog down toward the mailbox.

AUTHOR'S NOTE

Dear Reader,

Sometimes we experience an event so huge that it divides our time into *before* and *after*.

Before we moved away. After Dad left. Before Mom got sick.

For my family, that event was known as "the accident."

The summer I turned ten, on a road trip to visit my grandparents, a car skidded across the rain-battered highway and slammed head-on into our 1969 Chrysler. And the car behind us, unable to stop, plowed into the back of our car. The way Melanie describes the event to Dorit at their first sleepover is the way I still remember it happening.

My mother was critically injured and rushed to the hospital by ambulance. Our family was never quite the same.

Surgeries, doctor's appointments, curious stares at her bandaged (and unbandaged) face, and lingering health problems became not just her reality but our entire family's as well.

Years later, with much of her physical healing under control, she still suffered. A simple ring of the telephone or the doorbell caused her to jump as if someone had snuck up behind her. Our everyday comings and goings to work, school, and friends' houses scared her for our safety.

No one knew about PTSD, or post-traumatic stress disorder, back then. Melanie and Dorit understand that their parents—survivors of dangerous events, or *trauma*—have similar fears, but when I was younger, psychologists and doctors were just beginning to see the connections. Now we know that any life-threatening event—such as war, accidents, crime, or even a serious illness—can cause long-lasting effects on people's feelings of safety and security.

You're probably wondering what else in *Things That Shimmer* is true. The answer is, it's a mixture, like a soup where you first put in ingredients from the recipe but then add some that are your own idea. And after it cooks for a while, everything blends together into something new.

In middle school, I did have a best friend from Israel whose father fought in the Six-Day War. When Israel was attacked on Yom Kippur in the fall of 1973,

I saw it bring up fears in her family that I recognized. We realized that we had something huge in common, but we never talked about it.

As a writer, I imagined what it would have felt like to have those conversations with her, to have a best friend who understood what I was going through because she lived it too.

I also imagined what might tear best friends apart.

You might wonder why I set the story in the 1970s instead of in the present. I wanted to capture a moment in history when our country began to question our leaders. During the Watergate scandal, many people stopped believing that everything our elected officials told us was the truth. Removing them from office became a real possibility. The effects continue today. We all have a voice and can use it to hold our leaders accountable.

ACKNOWLEDGMENTS

So many people have accompanied me on this journey, which started so many years ago.

My deepest appreciation goes to . . .

My incredible agent, Susan Cohen, and her assistant, Nora Bellot, for seeing the potential in this story and helping me to bring it, and so many others, out into the world.

The Lerner/Kar-Ben team and cover illustrator Lara Paulussen, for understanding Melanie's heart from the outset.

Catriella Friedman and the rest of the team at PJ Our Way for awarding me with the author's incentive and for your belief in this project.

Jennifer Johnson-Blalock, whose deep insights and probing questions always encouraged me to dig deeper, and whose encouragement carried me along with kindness and care.

Deborah Brodie, of blessed memory, who read early drafts many years ago and whose sure eye led me in the right direction.

Liza Wiemer, for reading late drafts and for believing in this book with unwavering love and support.

Gretchen Will Mayo, whose evening writing class offered a creative lifeline when I was a young mother with a houseful of children, and who first said, "Bravo! You've written an excellent story!"

My dear, immensely creative, and talented friends in the Jewish kidlit community for your loving support, encouragement, generosity, and friendship. I am proud of who we all are together.

My father, Allen Weinberg, of blessed memory, who modeled a strong work ethic every day and taught me that work you love can bring great joy and meaning to your life.

My mother, Jean Weinberg, who filled my childhood with regular visits to our public library and never missed an opportunity to invite art, music, theater, and travel into our lives.

My family: Jay, Ari, Tova, Talia, Miryam, Tamar, and Saraleah, and the ever-expanding pack of grandchildren, for your love, encouragement, and interest (real or not!) in Watergate, Billie Jean King, John Denver, and all things of the 1970s.

And finally, to G-d, for the blessings I'm given every day.

ABOUT THE AUTHOR

Deborah Lakritz has worked as a social worker in schools, neighborhood centers, and family service agencies, helping people of all ages but mostly children. She is also the author of the picture books *A Place to Belong: Debbie Friedman Sings Her Way Home*; *Say Hello, Lily*; and *Joey and the Giant Box*. She lives in Milwaukee, where she and her husband raised their five children.